CHRISTMAS
AT THE
Pineview Inn

MOLLY GRAY

CHRISTMAS AT THE PINEVIEW INN

A Cozy Accidental Getaway Novel

MOLLY GRAY

To my parents, who missed their calling as professional Hallmark Christmas movie critics. I hope you enjoy this book full of small-town personality, perfectly timed snowstorms, and a bit of holiday magic (and yes, it ends exactly how you think it will).

Playlist

Santa Tell Me by Ariana Grande
Mistletoe by Justin Bieber
santa doesn't know you like i do by Sabrina Carpenter
Christmas Wrapping by Spice Girls
Santa Claus is Coming to Town by Lady Gaga
Merry Little Christmas by Robin Thicke
I'll Be Home for Christmas by Michael Bublé
Holiday Flight by John Williams
Sleigh Ride by Kelly Clarkson
Winter Things by Ariana Grande
Rockin' Around the Christmas Tree by Hanson
Let It Snow! Let It Snow! Let It Snow! by Frank Sinatra
Merry Christmas, Happy Holidays by Pentatonix

Jenni

Ankle-deep in shredded wallpaper, I'm starting to wonder what I did to deserve such punishment while helping my friends restore the Pineview Inn. My fingers are raw from pulling and scraping every wall throughout the inn over the past week. On top of that, my nasal passages are burning from the vinegar we've sprayed to loosen the decades-old paper adhesive.

This particular guest room was adorned with burgundy wallpaper featuring gold stripes, which had to go.

"Can you hand me that spray bottle?" Piper asks me. "There's a dry spot over here."

Piper's painter's jumpsuit is covered in dust and paint splatters, and you can tell she hasn't showered in a few days. Neither have I, since we've been working nonstop around the inn she and her girlfriend bought a few months ago. They are opening on December 22nd, and the inn needs to be in tip-top shape for the guests to enjoy a Christmas weekend getaway.

I toss the spray bottle to my best friend and remind myself that I love her. That's why I've been helping any chance I get, even though I'm not on the payroll.

"Did Niko have to scrape '90s wallpaper off the walls when he took over his resort?" Piper asks, her laughter echoing in the empty room.

My heart jumps a tiny bit at the mention of Niko, my long-distance boyfriend. "I highly doubt the Omorfiá was covered in tacky wallpaper, but right now, I'm hoping he had to at least polish the solid-gold fixtures. Otherwise, he had it way too easy."

Niko and I met earlier this year when I traveled to Greece for my job as a marketing assistant. My firm, Aspen Sky Marketing, was pitching our services to the board of directors at Niko's luxury resort, and I accidentally volunteered for the task. It's a long story involving a topless beach, a vindictive ex, and a lot of baklava. I came home from that trip with a promotion, the sweetest summer romance with Niko, and a newfound freedom from the cloud of self-doubt that had loomed over my career for years.

Since then, we have kept in touch, texting every day and calling when we can. But lately, I don't know exactly where we stand. Our romance was a whirlwind of sunshine, stolen kisses, and pure joy, so we never talked about what we both wanted long-term. Are we serious? Are we casual? Living on separate continents makes it hard to find time for meaningful connection.

Piper peels a considerable section of wallpaper off and tosses it to the floor. "When was the last time you guys spoke on the phone?" she asks, seeming to know what thoughts are swirling in my head. Piper has been subject to insufferable monologues as I try to figure out my relationship status, and she's handled it with endless patience.

"No, not really. He called me last night, but I fell asleep while he told me about meeting with a local environmental group."

That tends to be how it goes. Niko's mornings are usually quiet at work, so I try to stay awake in case he has a chance to call. I hate when I wake up with my phone on the pillow and realize I slept through our phone call, squandering our chance at connecting.

"That sounds like it's his fault. He should have been telling you everything he wants to do to you—"

"Nope." I put my hands up. "We are *not* having that conversation. I don't need a reminder of that particular long-distance challenge."

Piper squirts the vinegar solution my way, and I jump back. "You know you want to."

I try to laugh because Piper loves teasing me, but the attempt at levity catches in my throat.

"I miss him so much," I say, dropping to the floor, my back against the section of wall I scraped clean. "This has been so much harder than I thought it would be. I like him so much, but how can we build a relationship that has a future when we're two ships passing in the night?"

Nothing could have prepared me for the way my heart aches every time I miss a call. Or the excruciating emptiness of not knowing when I'll have another meaningful conversation with him.

"At least he'll be here for Christmas in a few weeks, right?" Piper says with a resounding cheerfulness. Piper might be the only person who is as excited about Niko coming as I am. She's counting down the days until she can meet the man who "saved" me in Greece. I returned as a very different person from that trip. One who was no longer chasing a dream that didn't fit, forcing myself into a box that was entirely the wrong shape for my life.

"He will. I need to stop wallowing and help you get this room ready." I get off the floor, dust myself off, and start scraping wallpaper again. My fingers scream at me, but making progress feels better than worrying about something I can't control.

Niko and I booked a room at the inn starting on opening night, so that we could support the girls, even though I have my own apartment now and no longer sleep in my childhood bedroom.

I wasn't very supportive when Piper told me they were buying the old inn where we both worked in high school. I'm pretty sure I said something stupid like, *"Why would you want to trap yourself in Pineview Springs like I did?"* Later, I felt like the worst friend ever. I had been unable to see her excitement because of the crap going on in my life. Luckily, Piper is one of the most forgiving people I have ever known.

Piper picks at the last bits of wallpaper in her section of the room. "Have you talked about what you and Niko are going to do after the trip? Where do things go from here?"

I have been avoiding that question for months since we decided to keep our summer fling going after I left the island. What *can* we do? His life is in Mykonos. Mine is here. It's as simple as that. I can't move there, with my family and job here. My U.S. citizenship is also a problem. I've already looked into the various ways I could live there, and they are neither easy nor cheap. Niko is a dual citizen and was raised in California before moving to Greece. He could eventually move here, but the hotel is his career. He's been really successful, and I would never ask him to leave it behind. He's also repairing a lifetime of dysfunction with his dad and supporting his cousin Ana, who lost her sister in a tragic car accident.

Sweet, amazing Ana. I miss her too.

"No," I finally admit to Piper. "We haven't talked about the future. And I'm too scared to bring it up. There's no good answer. Neither of us can leave our lives, so what other option is there? Traveling back and forth every few months?"

I don't want to think about what might happen if we don't figure out a better solution soon.

"That sounds exhausting," Piper says. She grabs a broom and sweeps up the wallpaper carcasses from the deep mahogany flooring. A couple of months ago, we pulled up all the carpet and discovered the most amazing hardwood floors underneath. They were in pretty good shape, having been protected by carpet all these years, but my dad and Piper's dad came in for a week to sand and refinish them. It was a labor of love, but totally worth it.

"I also don't think you should live in limbo. You need to ask him and figure something out."

"I know. I hate limbo. But what if he says he doesn't want anything serious?" I bite my lip, afraid to turn around and face her. I don't want to know the answer. I don't want to be stuck again, heartbroken and lost.

"I would be surprised if that were the case," Piper says. "But if he isn't serious, wouldn't it be better to know? So you can choose what you want for yourself?"

I know she's right, but it's so much easier to push it off and pretend a crossroads isn't looming in the near future, where Niko could decide I'm not worth the effort.

I run my hands along the wall, looking for bits of wallpaper that might still be clinging on for dear life. It gives me a minute to collect my thoughts, and I don't like the reality I'm confronting.

I have managed to hold back my tears, mostly, as I grab a corner of my shirt and wipe at my eyes to avoid the vinegar on my fingers. I made that mistake earlier, and my eyes still burn at the memory.

When I consider what I want to do about Niko, I'm frozen with fear. Sure, my life has turned around, and I know I'll be okay even if he doesn't want a future, but it would break my heart. Niko made me feel seen when I was at my lowest, and he still makes me feel like I can do anything.

I turn around. Piper is bent over, scooping wallpaper scraps into a black trash bag pinned between the toes of her work boots. I burst out laughing, feeling the tension in my chest loosen. "You look like you're digging for a lost bone. What are you doing?"

She squats down and wipes her brow. "It was some stupid life hack on social media. It's killing my back, though."

I retrieve the broom where she left it leaning against the door to the en-suite bathroom. "Why don't you hold the bag, and I'll sweep?"

"Deal," she says.

After a few minutes, we've cleaned up the bulk of the debris. We'll need to bring in the shop vac later and wash the walls with soap and water before painting, but it's good enough for now.

Piper puts her arm around my shoulder as we survey the room. "What is your gut telling you?"

I lean into her. "My gut is telling me I need to have a conversation with Niko because this can't go on much longer. It isn't fair to either of us to continue developing feelings without a chance of a future."

Piper squeezes me. "Having the tough conversation is the only way forward," she says. "You'll figure it out."

I hope so. I honestly don't know how, but there has to be a way. "Should we take these bags outside and check on Sarah?"

Sarah has been painting one of the other guest rooms by

herself while we've been in here. Her pop punk Christmas playlist reverberates through the floor boards.

"Good idea," Piper says. "We can help her finish painting."

As I trudge out to the gravel parking lot to toss our debris in the construction dumpster, my stomach fills with nerves at the thought of having a conversation with Niko. It feels too vulnerable and risky. I need to find a way to make a future a possibility before I bring it up with him. I need to be prepared.

2

Sarah

Surveying the room and everything I've set up fills my chest with warmth. *It's perfect.*

Piper has been stressed and weighed down by the renovations, and I want to treat her to a relaxing, romantic picnic, like the ones we used to have under the moon and stars in the middle of nowhere. As much as I love that we've settled down and taken on this challenge of opening the inn together, I want to make sure we don't lose touch with the wistful couple who spent years living in an RV and exploring the country.

Piper deserves to take her mind off things, and if I don't make sure she relaxes occasionally, she won't do it. I've been working overtime too, taking on extra graphic design clients to cover the bills while putting in endless hours at the inn. We both need a night off.

Earlier today, I went to the RV and retrieved our favorite

picnic blanket from our life on the road. I laid it out in the middle of an empty guest room with some pillows and lined the perimeter of the room with dozens of flameless candles to create soft, warm lighting. All I want is to spend tonight in her arms, not worrying about anything.

In the corner of the room, I fill an essential oil diffuser with nutmeg and pine. I turn it on low so that it will run while we pick up dinner. Hopefully, when we return and I open the door for Piper, it will smell like stepping into a Christmas shop.

I tiptoe out of the room, closing the door behind me, and creep across the landing to one of the other guest rooms where I've been touching up nicks in the baseboards and steaming the rug to lie flat. Once there, I pick up a heavy box of decor and make a show of setting it down loudly in the hallway.

"Hey Piper, are you getting hungry? Should we go pick something up?" I call down the stairs as I head to the front desk, where she should be doing paperwork.

"Is it that time already?" she asks, hunched over her computer, her eyes strained and shoulders tense. She needs this picnic more than I thought she did.

"It's a little after six, but if you're not at a good stopping point …"

She hasn't looked up at me yet. A tiny knot catches in my throat. I'm afraid we're drifting apart like this, so entrenched in the renovation that we don't see each other as more than business partners. I shake it off my insecurity and step closer.

I reach over and lower Piper's laptop screen. "Babe, you need to take a break or your eyes are going to melt out of their sockets. Let's go get some dinner, okay?"

Piper finally looks up, her eyes are red from exhaustion, her cheeks sallow.

"Yeah," she says, rubbing her eyes. "You're right. Let's go. I can finish this up later tonight."

Hopefully, we'll be doing something more fun than reading alcohol license regulations.

I grab our coats from the rack near the inn's large wooden front doors. "What sounds good? Thai? Pizza? Chinese? We can bring it home and eat here."

"Let's grab Chinese. We can have leftovers for lunch tomorrow."

Piper is always practical. That's one of the reasons I love her.

HALF AN HOUR LATER, we arrive back at the inn with our takeout in hand. "Let me just grab my laptop, and we can eat in the dining room," Piper suggests.

"Wait," I say, reaching out to stop her. "I don't want to work through dinner. I have something to show you."

Piper sighs. "Did something go wrong upstairs?" There's a heaviness to her words and defeat in her eyes.

"No, nothing like that. Come on, bring the food."

She follows me up the stairs to the second story. Standing outside of the guest room where I've set up the picnic.

"Close your eyes," I tell her, brushing a kiss to her cheek. I open the door and pull her into the room, dimming the lights and leading her up to the edge of our blanket. I take the food from her and set it down on the blanket.

"Okay, now open," I whisper, wrapping my hands around hers in the flickering light.

I don't know what I was expecting, but an exasperated sigh definitely wasn't it. Piper's shoulders slump as she looks around the room and finally meets my gaze. "Sarah, what is all of this?"

I open my mouth, and then pause, not understanding the question. "It's a Christmas picnic," I falter. "I thought it would be fun. I know it's still November, but once we get closer to Christmas, we won't have time to do anything special like this."

"Is it a special occasion? Why did you do all this?" Piper asks, sounding annoyed.

"It's a romantic dinner for the two of us," I laugh. Maybe she doesn't understand and thinks I'm suggesting we offer candlelit, mistletoe private dinners as some sort of honeymoon package. Actually ... that's not the worst idea.

"Sarah," Piper interrupts my daydreaming. "I don't have time for whatever this is. I have so much work to do before applying for our liquor license, and we have to have it by the opening."

I feel as if someone has stolen my ice cream cone and dropped it in the dirt. My defenses go up. "You can take an hour off to eat dinner and talk about something other than work with your girlfriend."

She scoffs. "No, I really can't. You don't understand. It's not just decorating. It's important paperwork that we won't be able to open without."

My throat tightens. I know the things I have been doing for the hotel aren't as important logistically. I grew up as the artistic daughter of two mining engineers. I understand where art stands in the hierarchy of importance. It still matters, though. An inn like this needs character. I've done the research. I've read the online reviews of our competitors and similar-sized mountain inns around the country. Every single five-star review mentioned how much people loved the little touches that gave the place character.

"I'm sorry. It was a bad idea," I mumble. This isn't a conversation I want to have. Arguing will only exacerbate her stress levels. "You should go downstairs and work. I'll clean this up."

I turn toward the corner of the room and start picking up candles, flicking the switch off at the bottom. It's very anticlimactic compared to blowing out real candles. I can't take my emotions out on a tiny black switch the same way. With my back to Piper, my cheeks prickle with embarrassment. I try to ignore her as she leaves, so it doesn't feel like such a slap in the face.

I hear footsteps over the soft music, which now feels decidedly unfestive, and let out a shaky breath. She's really leaving.

Of course, we can't take time out for a frivolous evening when we're about five weeks from our grand opening. I wipe a small tear from where it has fallen down my cheek. Just as I lean down to grab another candle, arms wrap around my waist and pull me. My shoulders tense at Piper's familiar embrace.

"I'm sorry," she whispers. "This was incredibly thoughtful. Can I have a do-over?"

I hesitate, struggling to find the right words. Can this evening be saved? Do I even want to?

"I don't know, Piper," I tell her. "You were right. We are way too busy for this. I didn't think it through. I just thought it would be nice to spend some non-work time together and remind ourselves why we are doing this renovation in the first place."

She takes my hand and pulls me to the middle of the room. My heart flutters in my chest. I don't know why I'm nervous. We've been together for almost ten years, but I still get butterflies when I'm feeling vulnerable. At this point, my heart is begging Piper for assurance that all is not lost. We aren't setting ourselves up for an endless winter of apathetic glances and quiet, passionless evenings spent in our own worlds. That can't be what we signed up for when we bought this place. We won't survive it.

"Sarah, I am never too busy to kiss my girl under the mistletoe," Piper says. "I'm sorry I forgot that. Please forgive me."

"Are you sure?" I ask, hating the thought of her staying and falling behind just so she doesn't hurt my feelings. I don't want a pity date or for her to resent me later.

Piper leans in and kisses me. There's a tender note of apology in her embrace, and I can feel the tension leaving my body. "Yes, I'm sure," she says, pulling away. "I should never have said those things. I have time for you, and what you do is important. I'm just exhausted and feeling the pressure of these licensing deadlines. Come on, let's eat before it gets cold."

"Okay," I say, making my way to the floor. I know how hard it is for her to take a break, so I give in and grab the bag of food. I pull out the takeout containers. "Chow mein for you and fried rice for me. Beijing beef, sweet and sour chicken ..."

"Did we get egg rolls?" she asks, searching through the bag.

I open one of the paper containers and hand over a roll. The fried wrapper flakes off onto the pads of my fingers. I start to wipe them on my pants, but Piper hands me a napkin. "Here, use this."

"Thanks," I mutter.

An awkward tension hangs in the air, neither one of us knowing how to move on from the argument. I can't wait to be on the other side of this opening, so Piper and I can get back to normal. I'm worried how we'll come out on the other side if we don't start remembering that we are a team.

3

Piper

The last time I was on Main Street, none of the holiday decor was up. The town was still entirely set in spooky season mode with pumpkins and scarecrows filling the door frames. Now, it's snowflakes, candy canes, and Santa hats. Real snow sits in pockets on the sidewalk, and fake snow is piled in window displays alongside nutcrackers and menorahs.

Walking down the street, I'm filled with nostalgia. I love seeing all of the shops dressed up for the festivities. It reminds me of the parades and town parties I grew up with. As a tourist town without a ski resort, Pineview Springs is busiest during the summer months, crowded with people looking for that rugged mountain experience. But during the winter, the town is just for us. We come together to celebrate and support one another's businesses during the slow winter months.

Well, most of us.

As I walk into the hardware store, I spot Charlie LeGrande near the front, and all feelings of nostalgia fly into the cold air outside. He's rambling on to the poor kid at the register, probably pining about the good ol' days if I were to guess. That's Charlie's modus operandi. Everything was better back in the 80s when the only people in town were miners and those supporting the mining community.

Before I can hear what he's saying, Charlie's eyes land on me, and his face transforms as if he's just smelled sour milk. "Well, look who the cat dragged in," he says. "If it isn't the Morris girl. I thought your family finally town?"

"Hi, Charlie," I say, knowing it's better to be nice than to get on his bad side. Keep him pacified. "How are you?"

"I've been better. It's way too dry this year. We're going to have a Christmas wildfire, like that one they had up in Boulder a few years ago. You watch. It's going to be bad."

And you'll find some way to blame it on anyone you don't like. Charlie retired from the mines a few years back, and from what I hear, he treats town commentary as a full-time gig nowadays. Jenni would tell me stories last year about all the things he complained about — from a new store opening on Main Street to the Fourth of July parade being rerouted. It's tempting to brush off his ramblings as those of an old man, but he has friends in powerful places. A whole generation looks to him for guidance. I don't want to give him any reason to consider me an enemy more than he already does.

I nod and head toward the tile section at the back of the store. One of the bathrooms at the inn has a handful of cracked tiles, so we've decided to replace the whole floor. I ordered tile and mortar online and watched five different DIY videos about the process, so I feel confident we can do it ourselves. I only need spacers, a notched trowel, and grout before we can tackle it.

As I peruse the options, Charlie continues to run his mouth

up front. Charlie was the manager of our town's largest mine for decades and was revered by almost everyone. He signed half the town's paychecks, so it makes sense. I think a lot of people, particularly the town's longest-standing residents, still feel like they owe him something.

My family moved to Pineview Springs from Texas when I was ten, and we were hated from the get-go. Dad's company came in with a lot of money and set up a river rafting operation, and a rental shop for kayaks, hiking gear and mountain bikes. Mountain tourism was surging at the time. Dad's company put a few local operations out of business, because they simply couldn't keep up with the demand. He tried to hire as many people who had lost their jobs as possible, but people blamed us for ever coming to town in the first place.

It was Charlie, in fact, who led a petition to kick my dad's company out of town when we first got here. He even ran for mayor to gain influence. The campaign was all about keeping Pineview Springs "local," with strong undertones that outsiders were ruining the mountain. Luckily, most people didn't want to oust the town's biggest money maker and Charlie lost the election. But his influence hung around. There was always a faction of people, Charlie included, who would rather never see anyone from my family ever again.

The worst part is that I don't always know who those people are. Just like any small town, people in Pineview Springs can be nice to my face, but vile behind my back — celebrate success in public while secretly rooting for failure. I have been burned by that type of behavior more than once when I thought someone was a friend, but then they turned their back on me when I needed them most. I'm terrified the same thing is going to happen with the inn.

Finding the correct size spacers, I mentally calculate how many I need and grab an extra package just in case before heading back toward the register.

Unfortunately, Charlie hasn't gone far. The poor teenage boy at the register is standing there like a deer in the headlights. I feel bad for him. He clearly doesn't know how to get rid of the old man.

"Hey, Charlie, mind if I sneak in and make my purchase? You must have important things to tend to around town, anyway, right?" I learned a long time ago that making people like Charlie feel important is the best way to keep them off my back.

"You never did answer my question, young lady. I thought your family left town a few years ago. Are you all back?"

I sigh. I'm surprised he hasn't heard about the inn, yet. He usually prides himself on knowing everything that happens in town. "My parents moved away a few years ago, but my girlfriend and I recently moved back. We're renovating the Pineview Inn."

"You?" he asks, rolling his eyes. "You took it over from the Harpers?"

"We did, yes."

"Just like your dad, then. Thinking you deserve to take over a local business and change everything around."

"It's going to be great, Mr. LeGrande," added the teen. "Everyone is excited."

Not everyone, I want to reply. I'm sure Charlie, and others like him, aren't so thrilled.

My mind flips back to a few weeks ago when I ran into a guy I knew from high school and his wife. She was a few years younger than us. Neither one of them went to college, choosing to stay here in Pineview Springs and work in town instead.

When I told them Sarah and I would love to have them come by the inn sometime for a meal, he gave me an uncomfortable look and said, "Yeah, maybe. We'll see."

It took me by surprise. He had always been nice enough in

school, and it wasn't as if I was asking them to book a room. It made me wonder if, after leaving for college, I have reverted to being an outsider? Will no one be excited that I'm back in town?

Charlie steps back from the register, and I'm relieved he appears ready to leave me alone. I set my items on the counter and pull my wallet out of my back pocket.

But Charlie stops short of the door. "Hasn't your family taken enough from this town?"

My heart shatters, but outwardly, I maintain the shield I've put up over the years. "I like to think I'm giving back to the town. The inn sat closed and empty for almost a year before we bought it."

He grunts and heads out the front door, the small bell ringing to signal his departure.

I bite my lips to keep my chin from quivering.

"Don't worry about him," the boy says. "He's always in here complaining about something or someone. I don't think anyone pays any attention to him."

I nod as he scans my items and the prices ring up on the register. "It's fine. I'm used to him."

It's a lie, but I have never known how to survive here without pretending that I'm not bothered by the likes of Charlie. I came back because I love this town, even if this town doesn't love me back.

Once my items are bagged, I head down the street toward Bobby's Café. I told Sarah I would pick up some BLTs for lunch. When I pull open the door and see Bobby at the counter, the hair on the back of my neck stands up. As if this morning hasn't been hard enough, Linda LeGrande, Charlie's wife, occupies the table closest to the register.

I guess it's true that one can't go anywhere in a small town without a run-in.

No one knows why Linda has stayed with Charlie all these

years. She always seemed nice enough, but how can she stay married to someone like him without sharing his beliefs? I don't trust her.

"Oh, Piper, hi," Linda says as I walk toward the counter. "I heard you were back in town."

Word spreads quickly. Had Charlie called her? Or had she heard from someone else and not given him a heads-up? "Hi, Mrs. LeGrande, it's great to see you."

I take a tentative step toward the register, hoping to end our conversation and place my order. But I'm not so lucky.

The woman—someone I vaguely recognize from Jenni's mom's knitting circle—sitting with Linda speaks up. "Linda, Piper is renovating the old inn! Isn't that nice? I bet it's going to be amazing."

I clench my jaw, a headache growing in the space behind my eyes. I would love to spend five minutes without someone expressing their expectations for the inn. The pressure is suffocating. Plus, the way she says the word "nice" sounds anything but.

"I had no idea," Linda responds, in a tone that's as fake as the jewelry around her neck. "I think that's wonderful. You're planning on making a few changes, I presume?"

I spin. "Not too many. We're preserving as much of the inn's original style as possible while updating amenities and adding some entertainment space. We're having a grand opening a few days before Christmas. You're welcome to stop by."

"Oh, I'll be there. You can count on it," Linda says with a grin. I can't tell whether she's being sincere or scheming to bring me down, just like her husband. Is she hoping to come and watch us fall on our proverbial faces?

I smile and nod, but I want to scream. I don't know why I ever thought this would be a good idea. The Harpers were supportive and excited when we talked about buying the inn.

They said they had been waiting for the right buyers, and we fit the bill. I guess I hoped their support would signal the rest of the town that we were okay. If any of these people turn on us, life here could be miserable.

I'm up next at the register, so I finally say goodbye to the two women and place my order.

"Don't worry about them," Bobby whispers after I pay, nodding toward Linda's table. "They just don't like change. Most of us are very excited about the inn."

I smile, half-heartedly. "Thanks, Bobby. I appreciate it."

4

Niko

The Omorfiá's head chef brings a steaming plate of keftedes to my table, and I'm immediately transported to childhood dinners at my yia yia's house in Athens during my annual summer visits. The juicy pork meatballs are covered in a creamy oregano sauce, served with pita bread and a lemon, parsley, and cucumber salad. Just the way she liked them.

Of course, I was supposed to visit my father on those trips, but I ended up at my maternal grandmother's house often when he traveled for work or some other function he found more interesting than his own child. Now, it feels like the past is repeating itself. I'm here in Greece, waiting for my father to fit me into his schedule. He was supposed to join me for dinner tonight, but something came up and he skipped his flight to the island. He says he'll be here tomorrow, but I'm not holding my breath.

At least our chef has finally come around to my desire to serve traditional, home-cooked fare in our on-site restaurant, rather than the upscale fusion dishes the resort used to offer. He's been asking me to come to the restaurant after hours about once a week to try a new recipe.

After my dad canceled, I invited my cousin Ana to join me. I hired Ana a few months ago as an events and community relations director, and I'm grateful for the company tonight. I'm tired of eating alone. I mostly spend my evenings alone in my office or trying to catch Jenni on the phone during her lunch break.

My flight to Colorado for the holidays can't come soon enough. Ten days and counting.

"Are you sure you don't want to come with me?" I ask my cousin.

Ana has been obsessed with America for as long as I can remember. She used to beg my mom to adopt her and bring her back home to California with us at the end of the summer. But instead of coming to Colorado with me for Christmas, Ana has insisted on staying behind to run The Omorfiá while I'm gone.

"Yes, I'm sure, Niko. Who else would be able to take care of this place the way I can?" she asks with a flip of her hair. Ana has always had a distinct confidence in herself, ever since we were kids. "Besides, if I'm there, Jenni will want to hang out with me instead of you, you big oaf."

Or maybe she's just a little arrogant.

"Okay, you don't need to name-call just because you're trying to steal my job," I accuse, pointing a fork at her. She laughs.

The keftedes are amazing. I wish Jenni were here. She would devour the entire plate. Watching her eat was one of my favorite things when she stayed at the hotel. She eats like it's a five-star experience every time. I remember when she tried baklava at our first meeting, and her face changed. She went from being anxious and fidgety to melting into her seat as if the world disappeared after that first sticky bite. Of course, the honey-induced serotonin wore off, and she bounced back into a nervous wreck. Eventually, though, we reached a point where she was comfortable being herself and no longer worried about the expectations of those around her. It was a beautiful transition.

"I could never steal your job," Ana says, wiping sauce from the corner of her mouth. "You still don't understand how grateful I am that you gave me a chance to work here, do you? This job changed my life, Niko."

I hate when she says that, like she didn't deserve it. Sure, I offered Ana the job, but she is kicking butt. There was something special about last summer, we all learned how to lean into our strengths.

Until coming to work at the hotel, Ana has been a glorified spokesperson for our family's wine empire. Our grandfather opened the first Psomas vineyard nearly sixty years ago. Then, my dad and uncle, Ana's father, took over the company and expanded our family name to more than 150 vineyards, 200 wine labels, and luxury wine-tasting experiences. Ana has modeled for advertisements, entertained at public events, and wined and dined the company's highest-profile clients—distributors, restaurateurs, and magazine editors.

She's never enjoyed being a walking sales pitch, but it was what her father expected of her. She didn't think she had a choice. When I offered her the opportunity to do something different, she seized the chance. Ana has organized weekly art workshops for our guests, charity galas, and community events. She's making a name for the hotel on Mykonos and working with Aspen Sky Marketing to make our hotel a top destination on the island.

"You'll do great. All you need to do is make sure everyone

on staff is accounted for so the hotel runs smoothly," I tell her. "And make sure the money is all moving where it should. We pay the food vendors weekly and the laundry service on the first of the month, so you'll need to take care of that, as well."

Ana nods, paying close attention. She's taking this seriously. Maybe a bit *too* seriously.

"One last thing I haven't mentioned, and no one knows I do this, is that every night I go to the storage closet in the back hallway behind the spa."

She nods again, her eyebrows pinched, waiting for more. This is *too* easy, I almost feel bad.

"I open up the cellar door, and … make an offering to the rats. As long as I bring them melon and fresh bread nightly, they leave the guests alone." I drop my tone even lower. "But if I miss a day, they get restless. You don't want to see what happens when they get restless." I keep my expression completely serious, while Ana's face moves quickly from fear and confusion to disgust and annoyance. She rolls her eyes at me. "I should smack you for that," she says.

I burst out laughing. "I'm sorry, I just couldn't help myself. You looked so serious," I apologize.

"It is serious!" She pouts.

"It's really not," I tell her. "Just pay the bills, and let everyone else do their jobs. It's not like it's high tourist season. We barely have any guests. You'll be fine."

"I know, but I don't want to mess this up."

I love how much she cares. Maybe I've grown apathetic. If something goes wrong, it's always fixable.

I take our plates to the kitchen. "It's not brain surgery, Ana. Truly. I'm not worried at all."

If I'm being honest, I would happily give her the entire thing. I don't own the hotel; my dad's company does, and I'm just the general manager. But I would turn that position over to her in a heartbeat. I took the job because I wanted to impress my dad, hoping it would lead to a better relationship if I did. But he isn't the relationship type. We only ever talk about work and the hotel. He has started to trust and respect my decisions as a general manager, but a father-son relationship is still nonexistent.

If I'm honest with myself, I don't think he wants one. I probably should have known, considering he never seemed to mind that my mom left him and moved me to the U.S. They were both so young and had the weight of family expectations on them, but he never made an effort. He never had more children, so I sometimes wonder if he even wanted to be a dad.

I've lost track of the times I've asked myself why I'm even here. Sure, it's been a fun challenge to take over the hotel and reimagine ways to serve the tourism industry, but it's not what I planned for my career. I didn't grow up dreaming of life on an island that goes dormant for a third of the year. It feels like I'm hibernating, waiting for life to start again in a few months when tourists start trickling off the boats and airplanes.

The thought of stepping down from the hotel feels like nailing the coffin shut on a relationship with my dad. If I walk away, he will not chase after me. I can guarantee it. Plus, I have built something great here with the staff and community. Moving on from the hotel feels like abandoning everyone I've worked so hard to support.

"What are you daydreaming about?" Ana asks. I didn't notice when she joined me at the kitchen door.

I shake my head. "Nothing," I respond. "Just tired."

"What did you think of the keftedes? Good enough for the menu?" she asks.

I nearly forgot that the chef will be waiting for a stamp of approval.

"I thought they were great, but what did you think? My opinion isn't the gold standard."

She considers before responding. "The meatballs were

perfection. But I don't think the cucumber salad is the best side dish for the entrée. Something a bit more savory would pair nicely."

I nod in agreement. "I'll let the chef know."

A few moments later, we walk into the quiet lobby of the hotel. In a few days, the lobby of the hotel will be transformed into a winter wonderland theme for our staff holiday party. Ana has been working tirelessly to celebrate the staff for all of their hard work this year. If it weren't for the party, I would have left for Colorado days ago. But the general manager should be there. Otherwise, what message would it send? That I care more about seeing a woman who was supposed to be a summer fling than the hotel? It's the wrong message, even if that's exactly how I feel.

I'm a jerk for wishing I could leave. Of course, I am happy to be here. I believe in the hotel and I'm proud of everything we have accomplished. I *should* be thrilled to usher in a new year of growth and success.

Instead, I'm dreading it.

Maybe I'm just missing the buzz of the summer season— the hotel filled with guests, the sun shining brightly through the halls, and new adventures every day. Winter on a destination island pales in comparison to the height of summer. Once things start to pick up in a few months, I'll get out of this funk.

I could convince Jenni to come out here for a couple of months in the new year. But she needs to be in the same general time zone as her clients, so they can reach her, especially at this early stage in her new position. I would never ask her to jeopardize her job. But I can't give up everything I've built because I miss her.

I need a better way to connect with her. We can make it work. I don't want to lose her or fail the hotel. We can make it work.

"What big plans do you have for Colorado? You never told me," Ana says, interrupting my spiraling thoughts.

"I'm letting Jenni take control of the planning, so I don't really know," I tell her. "We're going to help her friends open their inn, but I think she has a few adventures planned as well. I'd be happy going to the grocery store together. I just want to be with her."

Ana laughs. "I hope all your wildest dreams come true. Want to watch a movie tonight? Something sappy and festive?"

Ana loves movies, partly due to her obsession with moving to California with me and my mom.

I am not in the mood for sentimental happily ever afters when I'm in the middle of whatever is going on in my relationship. The worst part is that I am trying to keep a good attitude for Jenni. She worries about so much that I don't want to give her anything else to feel insecure about. So I pretend the distance doesn't bother me and everything is fine.

"Sure, your place or mine?"

"Mine, I have better snacks," she quips.

A couple of hours later, we're sitting on opposite ends of Ana's sofa as a generic stressed-out woman who left her hometown for life in the big city meets a rugged small business owner back home and questions all of her life choices.

"Do you think she ever ends up regretting it?" I ask.

"Regretting what?"

"Leaving her job and moving for the coffee guy," I say. "What if it doesn't work out?"

"Of course it will work out, they're in love!" Ana declares.

As the closing credits roll, I grab my phone to check the time. I know Jenni is out at a client site today, so I won't hear from her before I go to bed. I consider sending a text, but I don't want to distract her or make her feel bad that we haven't talked. I'll call her tomorrow night and try to catch her during her lunch hour.

"She obviously wasn't happy," Ana continues, sipping from her cup of tea. "He just helped her see that. So I guess, even if it didn't work out, she's still better off."

She's talking about the movie, but her words hit me like a freight train. I'm not happy here. I've been trying to convince myself otherwise, because I made a commitment. Am I really going to be happy here long term? And is the hotel really worth missing out on an opportunity to see where things go with Jenni? I shake my head. It's a movie. Not real life.

Still, I open my phone and send my dad a text, asking him to please make it to our dinner tomorrow. I have some things I need to talk to him about.

5

Jenni

My keys jingle as I climb the metal stairs up to the apartment I've been renting since I got my promotion. It's an adorable little loft above the souvenir shop on Main Street. It's perfect, not too far from my parents' house, and only a short bike ride from the inn. It has everything I need.

Most importantly, it's an apartment that I pay for with my own money. I can make my coffee however I like, stay up late without comment from my parents, and the knitting ladies aren't lurking downstairs to give me the Spanish Inquisition on my dating life.

As I reach the landing, I notice a white envelope with my name on it taped to the door.

I pull it down and rip open the letter, but my phone rings. The chime sends a surge of excitement through my veins. *Niko*.

I scramble through my bag trying to find my phone. I can't

miss his call. I always miss his calls. I dump the whole bag on the landing and grab my bright yellow phone case.

"Niko? Hi! I'm here!"

There's a brief pause on the other end. "There she is," Niko says, his voice low. I know he's teasing me, but it still makes me weak in the knees. Just like it did during our very first meeting at the Omorfiá Hotel. I blush at the recollection of that meeting. He ended up feeding me baklava and apricots, and I was smitten.

"How are you?" I ask, scooping everything back into my bag and grabbing my keys from where I tossed them on the floor.

"Amazing, now that I'm talking to you." My heart melts at the sound of Niko's voice. I have missed this so much. "What are you up to?"

I open the door to the apartment, throw my bag on the counter, and collapse onto the couch I got at a thrift store when I moved in. "I just got home from the library," I say. "As much as I hated it when I was forced to work there regularly when I was living with my parents, now that I live on my own, I miss it. "I had some research to do for a client, so I decided to get out of the house for a bit."

"That's great. No gum on the table, I hope?"

"Surprisingly, no. Just a toddler story time that got a little out of hand. What about you? How was your day?"

Niko sighs. He's been doing that often lately, and a tiny part of me worries that it's because he's getting bored. As much effort as Niko puts into staying in touch, I also know that he could have any woman in Mykonos. He's handsome and an all-around great guy. He does not have to settle for me. It must be getting tiresome waiting all day for me to wake up and contact him.

"It was good. Ana and I were in meetings all day securing

sponsors for our spring events. She asked more questions and got more guarantees than I would have."

He must be tired. That sounds like a long day.

"Do you have time to chat? I don't have any meetings. We could plan some things to do when you're here." My voice sounds desperate, which I hate. But at the same time, a girl deserves to sound desperate once in a while, especially when her boyfriend lives halfway around the world.

"Of course. I'd love to," Niko says. "I am going to dinner with my dad in a bit, but I have some time."

"Your dad? Good luck with that. What's the dinner for?"

Niko clears his throat. "Just some business moves to discuss. Nothing too big of a deal."

Hmm. Niko usually has some quip or complaint about his dad's antics. I want to ask what's keeping him quiet this time, but I would rather talk about our trip if our time is short. "How comfortable are you on ice skates?"

Niko chuckles. "Probably more comfortable than you are strapping into a parasail harness."

"Oh, my gosh," I say, indignantly. "I'm never going to live that down, am I? You could barely tell I was scared. I have an amazing poker face."

"You do, do you?"

I smile. Niko can read me like a book. It still surprises me how well he knows me sometimes, despite our short time together. From the first day we met at his resort, he somehow knew I needed a bit of fun in my life. Later, he told me he knew I was hurting, and he thought no one should be hurting in Greece.

"Okay, fine. You might have been able to tell I was terrified. *Might.* Anyway, do you want to stay in Pineview Springs the whole time or should we do a day trip somewhere like Breckenridge?"

I can't wait for him to meet Piper, Sarah, and my family,

but I'm also hoping to steal him away for some one-on-one time. After being separated for months, we need time together. Time for us and time to discuss our future, as terrifying as that may seem. I know we'll need to have an honest conversation, which is not something I am used to. The only way to do that is to be on our own.

"Just the two of us?" Niko asks with a note of hope in his voice, reading my mind.

"Just the two of us." I smile broadly, even though he can't see me.

"That sounds amazing. I can't wait to see you."

"Me neither," I say, and hesitate. I bite my lip before continuing. "Also, my mom keeps asking which night we can come over for dinner. They'll be in Seattle visiting my brother when you first get here, but all three of them are flying back a few days before Christmas."

"I was hoping I would get to meet them," Niko says. "Really, I'm all yours. Put me to work at the inn or drag me all over Colorado. Either way, I'll be happy."

My confidence grows with every word. If he's this excited to visit me, he must want a future. "Now that you mention it," I say. "Piper is still looking for a dish boy."

"Like I said, if you're there, I'm game to wash dishes." Niko clears his throat. "Look, I need to run. My dad just texted and he's landed early. I'm so sorry. If it were any other night, I would blow off dinner, but this is important. I'm glad I caught you, though, even for a few minutes."

My heart drops. Another stunted phone call.

"Oh … of course. Yeah, I should probably finish up a few things here anyway. But I miss you."

"I miss you, too," Niko says. "So much. Things are going to get better soon, I promise."

We hang up, and I look around the apartment. I love this

place, and everything it represents about getting my life back on track, but right now it feels lonely.

I grab my bag from the kitchen and take it to the table. When I pull out my laptop, the letter from earlier flutters to the floor. I stoop to grab it and finish pulling it out of the envelope. I skim it as I stand at the table. It's a letter from the landlord reminding me that my apartment lease is up at the end of December, and I'll need to be out. When I moved into the apartment, I knew it was a sublease and that the renters would be returning in the new year. But I had forgotten about it, with how busy I've been.

I open my computer and type in the leasing website to browse other apartments in the area when my phone pings.

> Niko: Just thinking about you. Wish you were here.

I stare at the phone and wonder for the thousandth time why, when I finally find a good man, he has to live on the other side of the world. But Niko is worth it. People like him don't come around every day.

> Jenni: I wish I were there more!

I turn my attention back to the computer, but burgeoning tears blur my vision. What is wrong with me? This should be an exciting moment, searching for my next apartment, but all I feel is dread that doing so will lock me here, while Niko is in Greece.

I don't have any other options. My life is here. My job is here. Niko's job is in Greece. I can't do anything about it.

Maybe, once I find a place, I'll feel more settled. Once it's final, I won't worry about whether I'm doing the right thing. My choice will have been made, and my fate will be sealed.

Right?

But with each apartment listing, I feel increasingly anxious, as if I'm making a mistake. I pull out my phone and re-read our messages from the last few days, pausing on the last one Niko sent.

Niko: Wish you were here.

I have researched moving to Greece about a dozen times. I could stay as a tourist for a few months, but no longer without a visa. I could qualify for a digital nomad visa, but it requires a lot of paperwork, Amber's approval, and figuring out the tax situation, which is something I don't see happening. I can't make that commitment yet. Besides, am I willing to leave behind the life I've started rebuilding?

All I wanted after everything fell apart was to get back on my own two feet. And once I realized that the fast-paced life I had been chasing in Chicago wasn't right for me, I embraced my newfound independence in Pineview Springs. I'm thriving. Wouldn't pausing everything be just another setback? Giving up the life I've built for some guy?

But Niko isn't just some guy. I learned last summer that sometimes what feels right looks wrong on paper. Maybe doing whatever I can to be with him is the right choice, even if it means giving up my hard-earned independence.

I open my message thread with Amber.

Jenni: Can we talk sometime this afternoon? I have a favor to ask you.

Amber: Sure! I'm free now.

Now? My chest tightens. Why does she always do this to me? She loves to unknowingly push me into the deep end as soon as I even consider dipping my toes in the water. I wanted to put together a persuasive argument before we talked.

Amber is technically still on maternity leave, but she stays in touch almost daily to ensure everything at the marketing agency she built from the ground up is running smoothly. I might not be able to reach her later, so it's now or never.

She picks up on the first ring. "Hi! What can I do for you?" Amber asks.

"I know you're coming back from maternity leave soon, so I'll be handing a lot of my clients back over to you. I was wondering, after that happens, if I could maybe take some time off. A month or so, something like that?"

The words come tumbling out of me in a way that would have horrified me six months ago, but I'm more comfortable with Amber now. I know she'll consider things reasonably. She won't say no just for the sake of it. I realized I'm lucky to have Amber as a boss when I was in Greece the first time. When I ran away from the big pitch meeting I had been working toward, I expected Amber to fire me on the spot. Instead, the first words out of her mouth were concern for my well-being.

"Is everything okay?" she asks. "You don't have to tell me anything personal, but is there a reason you need this time off that I could help you with?"

"Do you remember the hotel in Greece we signed?"

"You mean, do I remember when you volunteered for an assignment above your pay grade, freaked out, and then totally nailed it?"

I laugh. "Uh, yeah. That one."

"Go on…"

"Well, when I was there, I connected with the general manager," I tell her. I don't know why I'm saying all of this. Maybe I am looking for some reassurance, or for her to talk me out of this if it's a preposterous idea. "We have kept in touch, and I think we have something special. But I need to spend more time than two weeks with him to know."

"You are dating a client?" Amber asks. Her words lash out like a whip.

"I—well, sort of? I know I should have told you sooner, but I promise we've kept everything above board. I've never touched his account or tried to influence the work in any way." My heart is pounding, but laughter erupts from the other end of the phone.

"I'm sorry, that was just too good an opportunity. Of course, I know. Niko couldn't stop gushing about you when I called to welcome him to Aspen Sky. Something obviously happened."

Relief floods my body. I didn't think we were being obvious, but at least she doesn't sound angry anymore. "So, it's okay that we're together?"

"You probably should have disclosed it sooner, but from what I can tell, you have both been professional. I think it's fine. As long as you don't break his heart, causing him to turn around and sue us for some fabricated issue."

A nervous laugh escapes me. "I doubt it's possible for me to break *his* heart, but regardless, Niko would never."

"The way I see it, I'm taking my client load back in the new year, and since you don't have your own client list yet, this is as good a time as any to take a short sabbatical. You have to promise me you'll come back, though."

"Oh, my gosh. Thank you so much! You have no idea how much I appreciate this. I promise I'll make it up to you."

"You have already done so much while I've been on leave. You've earned this. But speaking of babies, I've got to go. It seems like his nap time is up."

Amber hangs up, and I gleefully return to my laptop. With a sigh of relief, I close out of the realty website. If I'm going to Greece, I'd rather just put my stuff at my parents, save on rent, and then find another place when I get back.

In a new tab, I open a flight finder site. I know exactly what I'm going to wrap up for Niko on Christmas morning.

Goodbye two-minute phone calls, and hello to long, romantic walks on the beach.

6

Piper

PINEVIEW SPRINGS, COLORADO
LATE NOVEMBER

"I can't shake the fear that people aren't going to support us and that all of this work is going to be in vain," I say, before dipping my brush into a can of white paint.

A dark cloud of uncertainty has been looming as we get closer to the opening of the inn. Yesterday's run-in with Charlie LeGrande felt like a hailstorm. I've been trying to pretend I'm okay, but he finally broke me, and I need Jenni and Sarah's reassurance. They both know how awful my first few years were here, but I'm still embarrassed that I can't get over this fear about the inn.

All three of us are working in the lobby today, freshening up the paint on all the trim. Sarah is manning the painter's tape, while Jenni and I paint. It's the last room, and the finality of it has brought my fears into full view.

"What do you mean?" Jenni asks, looking up from where

she's sitting cross-legged, hunched over the baseboard with a brush in her hand. "The inn is going to fill up with guests as soon as we open. I've already got ads running, and we're seeing great click-through."

Jenni is handling all of the marketing efforts pro bono. We work at the same agency, and I trust her to do the job, but it's been weird not being involved when that's what I do for a living. She and Amber agreed that I shouldn't market my own hotel and insisted that we don't pay until the inn is making a profit.

I argued at first, but I've been way too busy sanding, painting, and landscaping. I have loved the hands-on work. This feeling of getting my hands dirty, building something meaningful, was missing in my life when we were on the road.

"Not the guests ... the community," I respond. I'm not worried about getting customers into the inn. We've put in so much work that this place is fantastic. But a community like ours doesn't always like change or outsiders, as Charlie proved yesterday.

Jenni hesitates.

"Well?" Sarah asks, fidgeting with a roll of blue painter's tape. I didn't tell her about my run-in at the hardware store. I didn't want to scare her because she's already as nervous as I am.

"I think there will be an adjustment period because new things are hard," Jenni says. "But the community will come around. They always do."

I massage a cramp in my hand from the hours of painting. "I hope so. We have just changed so much. What if people get defensive of the way it used to be and want to run us out of town?"

The inn's property was always a forested, natural area with a few benches scattered throughout. Earlier this fall, I tore down a lot of the gnarled trees and foliage and poured a concrete patio. We built a massive outdoor fireplace, installed long wooden tables, and created a grassy area for games, like bocce ball and cornhole. We are working on obtaining a liquor license and plan to host a beer garden in the summer months, offering an array of outdoor activities.

Take all of the wallpaper we've replaced, the new artwork Sarah has been collecting, and the furniture we've replaced, it's a lot of change. Sarah has been a visionary when it comes to the decor, something I could never do. But what if everyone thinks the old way was better?

"Honestly, Mrs. Harper would use her teacher voice on anyone who criticizes you," Jenni says. "She wants the two of you to make this place your own. Where is all this worry coming from?"

Her face is full of concern and sympathy. But I'm honestly surprised she doesn't understand. I look at Sarah, the beautiful, creative, eccentric love of my life, and wonder why I ever wanted to open us up to the type of trauma I experienced as a child, moving here. "I think I am just scared of rocking the boat. I don't want a repeat of the past."

Ever since my run-in, more incidents from the past have resurfaced in my mind. Girls who laughed at my Texas accent, adults who talked about my parents ruining the town, and teachers who treated me differently from my classmates. I thought I had stopped caring when I went through a spunky teen phase and moved away to college — but the pit in my stomach tells a different story.

Deep down, I'm terrified of being that little girl again. "I just don't want things to go the way they did for my dad, that's all."

Jenni comes to my side, taking the paintbrush from me. "Piper, that will never happen. That was years ago, and the town has grown. This is a completely different situation."

"And we're in this together," Sarah adds. "You don't have

to carry it alone. I'm sorry I haven't been more aware of how you're feeling."

I shrug. I don't want her sympathy. I want to be strong for her and not care what anyone else thinks. I should be a provider, not a worried mess. I want everything to work out for us, but I have never been able to predict or control the town's reaction, and that terrifies me.

"It's fine. Like Jenni said, it was ages ago." I squeeze Sarah's hand. "And she's probably right. The town will love everything we've done here because you have such an artistic eye."

"And you are the perfect person to make it all come to life."

Jenni clears her throat, reminding us she's still here. "I get you're the perfect couple, but could you please take mercy on a girl whose boyfriend is a million miles away right now?"

Just for that, I give Sarah a huge kiss, exaggerating every sound.

"Okay, that's it, now I'm really walking out." Jenni puts her hands up.

Sarah immediately pushes me away and begs her to stay. "No more PDA, we promise," she says.

Jenni picks up her paintbrush, runs her pointer finger along the edge, and then flicks it at me, covering my face in tiny white dots.

"Okay, I deserved that," I tell her. "Let's get back to work. I'll buy you a drink later."

I take a breath and return to the windowsill. I hope Jenni is right. Because I don't know if I can bear the town turning on us. I need to protect Sarah.

"Do you know what I wish?" Sarah asks as she rips a strip of tape for the last window in the room. I expect her to make some grand declaration about belonging, but she surprises me by completely changing the subject. "I wish we could put a little bookshop at the inn." She points to the corner of the lobby that we plan to use for a coffee bar and water station. "Wouldn't it be adorable? We could sell cozy little mysteries set in the mountains, and travel books ..." Sarah trails off, a whimsical look on her face.

I sigh, dropping my shoulders. A bookshop? We don't have the space, the funds, or any knowledge of the book industry. This is just another far-fetched idea that I'm going to have to snuff out.

"That's an interesting idea," I say, cautiously. I don't want to hurt her feelings by squashing the idea right off the bat.

Sarah's brows furrow, her eyes dropping to the floor. "I know. I know, it's not practical. I was daydreaming out loud," Sarah says. I bite my lip, feeling guilty.

"I really do love it," I plead. "You have the best ideas, but we can't do that now. In a few years, when we're up and running, we can figure something out. We need space and time."

"I know," Sarah says and turns toward the window she's working on. Effectively telling me that she's done talking. "Last strip of tape here, then I'll go clean up in the kitchen."

I should say something, but I don't have the words. Instead, I stand frozen and watch her rip off the last piece of tape and exit the room without a backward glance.

When Sarah has left the room, Jenni sets her paintbrush down on a sheet of plastic and sits on the floor next to me.

"Arms getting tired?" I ask.

"No, I'm good. I just thought you might want to talk about whatever just happened between you."

I sigh and lay my brush down across the top of the paint can. "Do you think she's mad?"

"I don't think she's mad, but I do think she's hurt. Maybe Sarah just wants you to daydream with her. She knows it's not practical to sell books on opening day. That's why she said she *wishes* she could open a bookshop. I think she needs you to keep the magic alive a little bit while she daydreams, rather than pulling the rug out from under her."

Keep the magic alive? My brain doesn't operate that way. My first instinct has always been to focus on logistics. It's even worse now that we're trying to get a business off the ground.

"I don't have the mental capacity for magic right now. We're running behind on getting this place put together, and I'm still working full-time at Aspen Sky on top of it."

Jenni grabs my forearm. "I know, and Sarah gets it. Just try to be a little more generous in your response next time. Of all of the daydreams I've heard, this was actually the most practical."

I chuckle as I remember Sarah's idea to build a pool and sauna beneath the inn. Or the time she suggested a rooftop bar, even though we don't have a flat roof. A bookshop isn't actually all that bad.

"True," I say. "It's better than the reindeer petting zoo idea."

"No ... she didn't! When?"

"She did! The other night as we were going to bed. I think it was mostly a joke, but you never know with her."

"I love her," Jenni says, her eyes crinkling at the corners.

"Me too," I smile.

As we finish painting, I wonder if the bookshop really could be the idea that I make work for her. It only needs to be a few shelving units and a cash register. I could find space somewhere and figure out how to source the books through a wholesaler or distributor. We should make back the cost if we do it right.

The Pineview Inn Bookshop. It does have a certain appeal.

7

Sarah

DENVER, COLORADO
EARLY DECEMBER

I stare at the black and white checkered floor of a queer-affirming barbershop in Denver and can't shake a feeling of restlessness.

I found a home furnishing store that sells the perfect blankets for the guest rooms at the inn. When I mentioned going to get them, Piper said she would come along to get her hair cut. We still haven't found someone in the mountains who understands her masculine style. It's not quite a men's haircut, but definitely not something you can get at a women's hair salon with curlers, platinum dyes, and dryers out of the nineties.

Usually, I wouldn't mind sitting and waiting for Piper, but today I can't stop fidgeting. It's ridiculous. Maybe it's because there is so much to do back at the inn, or perhaps I can't wait to get my hands on the comforters I found. They were sold out online, but it said they had plenty in store.

I can't wait to get them to the inn and style each room. I have tons of fabric to make pillows, little decorative pieces to style, and pictures to hang. My brain is racing a hundred miles an hour, and I can't calm it down. I would read to keep my mind occupied, but I forgot my mafia romance at home.

"Hey Pipe, what if I head over and get the blankets? Then I can swing back around and pick you up."

Piper glances up from her phone, no doubt checking our bank account and the calendar ad nauseam. "Are you sure that's a good idea?" she asks, a teasing glint in her eye.

Piper knows I can't be trusted in a mall. I get distracted easily and can't always tell myself "No" when I see something I want. Like the cute stuffed moose I saw last week, and suddenly *needed* for the front desk. But this should be easy because we already know exactly which quilts we want. I'll walk in, grab ten of them, and head to the register. Simple. Easy.

"Yes, I can handle it. I promise," I say. "I can't sit still any longer. I'm crawling out of my skin."

"Okay," Piper says, grabbing my hand and planting a kiss on my lips. "I'll see you when you're done."

I leave her to wait for an open chair and drive a mile or two to the mall. Once inside, I'm struck by the particular nostalgia of a mall at Christmas time. Ariana Grande's version of "Last Christmas" plays softly from the overhead speakers, and Christmas trees adorned with tinsel and twinkle lights line the walkways.

In the middle of the food court, a small motorized Christmas train is giving children rides to Santa, and everyone is clad in winter coats, scarves, and frenzied energy reserved only for holiday shopping. At least I'm festively dressed in a green corduroy skirt and gold sweater.

I haven't thought about what to get Piper for Christmas. We talked about not doing gifts this year, but I hate the idea of not having something for her to unwrap. She deserves something.

This year has been challenging, and I want to remind her how much I love her. She's the mistletoe to my fresh garland, the frosted glass to my festive window display, and I can't imagine life without her. Even when I'm antsy and agitated about waiting for her hair appointment, I wouldn't want to wait for anyone else in the world.

I stop at a mall directory with a giant ribbon wreath to find my way to the store. It's on the opposite side of the mall on the second story, so I start walking, excited to be able to window shop along the way.

I peek into toy shops and clothing stores, but when I walk past the candle shop, I allow myself two minutes to smell all of the Christmasy pine and cinnamon scents. My favorite is the gingerbread and vanilla candle. And we do need candles for the front desk. We can't have a Christmas opening without Christmas candles filling the lobby with a cozy glow.

Twenty-ounce candles are part of a "buy two, get one free" sale. I grab six different luscious wintery scents. Piper can't be mad about a purchase under $100. That's basically discretionary spending compared to everything else we've purchased lately. And they are a necessity. Sort of.

I hold the candles in my hand, running a finger over the embossed gingerbread men on the label. It can be my early Christmas gift to her. Then she really can't argue. I have listened and agreed every other time she's told me something isn't in the budget. I check out and take my candles with me.

I won't purchase anything else extra. In fact, I walk straight past my favorite sneaker emporium where a rainbow display of Converse shoes screams, "Try me on! Buy me! Look at all the colors!" I don't even give them a second glance.

Finally, I arrive at the home goods store. Excitement fills

my chest like steam from a hot cup of tea, swirling and whimsical.

The front of the store is filled with holiday bedding, throw pillows, and dish sets. The reds, greens, and golds would make the inn so incredibly festive. My favorite are the pillows with snowmen with embroidered ribbon scarves that flutter off the pillow itself. And imagining the Christmas plates with hand-painted sleds and snow-covered pine trees in our little dining room is almost too much for my cheer-filled heart to take. But I walk past them, holding strong.

I head toward the back of the store, looking for the green, blue, and yellow patchwork quilts featuring appliquéd pine trees and black bears. When I found them online, I knew nothing could be more perfect for the Pineview Springs Inn. And miraculously, Piper approved of the price tag.

I scan the floor-to-ceiling shelves full of bedding sets. I see pink quilts, black and white flowery quilts, neutral tones, and ombré spreads, but not the ones I need.

I head to another wall where throw blankets hang from brass rods. I run my hand along the cashmere, wool, and flannel blankets, but strike out again on the black bear quilts.

"Can I help you find something?" a bubbly middle-aged woman asks. She's dripping with Martha Stewart coziness and is exactly who I'd expect to work here. I wouldn't be surprised if she started passing out freshly baked chocolate chip cookies.

"That would be great. I'm looking for a quilt. I think it's called the Laurel? It's blue and yellow and has pine trees on it."

She crosses her arms over a bright red apron and thrums her fingers. "Oh! I remember that one! We sold out of that weeks ago."

I open my mouth in confusion. "But the website said you had a lot in stock?"

The woman looks at me with pity in her eyes. "I've been trying to tell management that the website never updates. I'm so sorry, dear. We are definitely sold out. Can I check other stores for you? We have a few Colorado locations."

It's just my luck that the blankets were sold out, but it's worth a shot to check other locations. I don't know if I can convince Piper to drive very far, but maybe Jenni would come with me. That would be fun.

"Yes, thank you," I tell the woman. I follow her to the register. She types a few notes into a computer as Michael Bublé croons overhead that he'll be home for Christmas. My mind is racing to figure out what other options we'll have for quilts. Nothing else in this store looked remotely right for the inn.

"How many do you need? Just one?"

"No, ten actually."

She laughs. "Ten? How big is your house?"

"Actually, my girlfriend and I are opening a small inn up in the mountains. These are for the rooms."

"How lovely! Where is it?"

"Pineview Springs. It's a little town south of Breckenridge."

"South of Breckenridge? Must be tiny." She types a few things into her computer and grabs the mouse, her frown deepening with each movement.

"The closest store with any in stock, according to our internal system, is in Vegas. Can I call them for you and verify how many they have?"

I briefly consider a road trip to Vegas. But even if they have enough in stock, that would be a two-day journey. I can't spare that amount of time away from the inn.

"No, that's okay. Thank you, though."

"I'm sorry again for the inconvenience. Let me know if you want to look at anything else, and good luck with your opening!"

I leave the store, dejected. I had my heart set on those blankets. Piper wants to order plain white ones from a hotel supplier, and now she'll probably say this is a sign that we should go that route. I cringe at the thought. I am not ready to settle for boring white bedspreads. I can find something in time.

I walk back to the other side of the mall where I entered, hoping more window shopping will lift my mood. I wander past the LEGO store, but even their brand-new holiday sets aren't enough to break me out of my funk. I should probably give in and order white blankets. A good business owner would put practicality above artistry, but the thought breaks my heart.

I pull out my phone to text Piper that I'm on my way back when I walk past a jewelry store, and the most beautiful ring I've ever seen catches my eye. It's a thin black gold wedding band with two rows of diamonds and blue sapphires around the entire ring. It's precisely the style of ring I've always imagined Piper wearing—elegant, dark, and simple. I can't pull my eyes away from it. I drop my phone in my purse without another thought.

It's like the first time I met Piper. I grew up in an even more rural town than Pineview Springs and didn't have many friends at my small K-12 school. Once I got my driver's license, I started driving to Pineview Springs often to meet people. One day, I decided to try the rock-climbing gym. I walked into the gym and saw Piper belaying one of her guy friends. My heart did somersaults when I laid eyes on her. I knew I was attracted to women at that point, but I had never met an actual, real-life girl who lit my insides on fire the way I saw romance happen in the movies. I couldn't take my eyes off her during my beginner's lesson, and afterward, I introduced myself. The rest is history.

And now, I can't look away from this ring.

Piper and I have discussed getting married someday in the future, but we never put any solid plans into place. Maybe that's what we need right now. We own the inn together, and we're settling down. If now isn't the right time, when will be?

I walk into the store. "Excuse me?" I ask the first jeweler I see. "Can I see the diamond and sapphire wedding band in the front window?"

"Of course, let me get it for you," he says.

As soon as he hands me the ring, it sings in my hand. This ring is a sign. It has to be.

I *need* to propose to Piper with this ring for Christmas. I can feel it in my bones.

"How much is it?" I finally remember to ask. Considering that our bank account is depleted and our credit is tied up in a business loan, I'm scared to hear the answer.

"This is 18-karat black gold with a row of colorless diamonds and deep blue sapphires. It was hand-crafted right here in the shop," he tells me, holding the ring up to the light. It sparkles.

Yes, yes, I know. Just tell me if I have a snowball's chance in hell of affording it.

"It's $2,950 if you buy it during our Christmas sale. It's normally $3,699, but all rings and necklaces are twenty percent off right now."

My stomach clenches. We do not have that kind of money right now. And there's no way that I can ask my parents for help after they just helped us with the down payment for the inn. Reluctantly, I hand the ring back to him, feeling as if I'm turning over my heart and soul.

"Okay, thank you. I'll need to think about it."

He nods and puts the ring back. "Come back anytime. The sale runs until Christmas Eve."

I push my sleeves up to my elbows as I exit the jewelry store. I have to find a way to make three grand in the next few weeks. We don't have that kind of money in the bank right now with the renovation costs, but nothing is going to stop me from getting that ring. There's a pep in my step that wasn't there earlier, as I daydream about all of the ways I can propose.

When I get back to Piper, she is done with her haircut, looking beautiful in an asymmetrical fade, her black hair swooping down on only one side. My heart aches at seeing her, blissfully unaware of the perfect ring that just slipped through my fingers.

"I've got good news and bad news," I tell her.

"Well, I think I'll take the good news," Piper laughs. "What happened?"

"I got some candles for the lobby that smell like a Christmas bakery bottled up and infused into wax. They were on sale!"

Piper rolls her eyes with a smile. "Okay … what's the bad news?"

"Well, I stayed way under budget on the quilts, which I know sounds like good news, except it's because they were completely sold out."

Piper runs a hand through her freshly cut hair. "I'm sorry. I know you loved those. Should we order the white ones so you can stop worrying about it?"

I knew that's what she would say, but I'm not giving up that easily. "Just give me two more weeks. I'll find something else."

Piper purses her lips. "Fine, two weeks. Nothing more."

"I'm on it, don't worry," I tell her as we make our way to the car. As we drive back up the mountain, I scroll through bedding websites, bookmarking anything that catches my eye. But more than one, I find myself clicking onto a new tab and pulling up the jewelry shop to admire the ring I saw, and my heart flutters with anticipation.

8

Niko

After the movie last night with Ana, I knew I had to do something about my life. I was up half the night, deep in thought. I ran every scenario over and over in my mind, listing out all of the pros and cons. After hours, I finally settled on a plan that I know will work. I just have to convince my dad, and then I can get the ball rolling.

So, I put on my best suit, picked his favorite restaurant, and am hoping for the best.

I arrive, and the hostess seats me at a table for four in a quiet area of the restaurant. Surrounded by empty tables, I wonder if it would have been better to have people around so he can't be too brash or emotional. My dad is known for his fiery personality when it comes to business. If he's passionate about something, it shows.

I wave down a waiter to ask if we can move tables, but it's

too late, my Dad is entering the restaurant with all the confidence that comes easily to a man of his accomplishments. Dad is the type of person who can walk into any meeting and know he's in control. That's why this is going to be difficult.

Dad sees me and waves. He's clearly in a good mood, and I can't decide if that's a positive sign or not. It could make him more amenable, but he could also refuse to listen to me because he's focused on whatever good news drew that smile on his face.

"My son," Dad says. "It's good to see you. Please, don't stand on account of me. Sit, sit."

I'm unsure what to make of all this. Clearly, he's making an effort, which doesn't happen often. I don't know why or how he'll react to my news when it's finally time to tell him, especially on a rare day when he isn't brushing me off for something wine-related. I don't think my decision would be any different even if he had spent more time on our relationship while I've been living here. It would have been nice, though.

"I've ordered us a bottle of Xinomavro," I tell him, knowing that the island's finest Greek red wine was the safest choice. "But if you'd like a white, we can switch for a Malagousia."

"A great choice," he says, picking up a menu. "But if we're celebrating, we can add some cocktails later." Dad winks at me. He has never done that before in my entire life. Whatever has him in such a good mood might actually work to my advantage. If he's this excited about whatever it is, maybe he won't care that I'm leaving.

"How was your trip, Dad?" I ask, as we both peruse the menu. I'm sure my father knows exactly what he wants, but the butterflies in my stomach are interfering with my appetite, and I can't make up my mind.

"It was horrible. I only got one drink for a forty-five-minute flight. Only one," he says, extending his pointer finger and looking at me with eyebrows raised, and then chuckles. "But what was I going to do? Andres is using the company jet in Ibiza."

I resist the urge to roll my eyes. Of course, he would complain about something like that. I would bet this man hasn't flown commercial in twenty years.

The waiter arrives and we place our orders. Dad has a handful of modifications for his order—not because he has any allergies, but because he thinks he's important enough to request complete personalization.

"Just the kleftiko for me, please. Thank you," I say, handing the waiter my menu. The slow-roasted lamb will be good with the wine. I had planned to talk with Dad about my decision after we ate, but I don't think I'll be able to take a single bite until I get this off my chest.

I take a deep breath. I need to make this news as palatable as possible if I want to salvage anything from our relationship. Of course, he can't make me stay and work for him. But I would rather not get on his bad side, either.

"Dad, I would like to talk to you about my future at the hotel," I start. "I have learned so much in the year-and-a-half since I've taken over as general manager."

Dad nods, barely concealing a smile. He is acting strangely. I'm really not sure what to make of it. "Yes, son. I've been waiting for this day."

He's been waiting for me to quit? That's harsh, even for him. "I don't understand. What have you been waiting for?"

A smile spreads across his face now. "I've been waiting for you to realize that your place isn't at the hotel."

That clarified nothing. "Where do you think my place is, Dad?"

The waiter brings us our pita bread and olive hummus appetizer.

Dad takes a slice of bread and digs into the hummus before

responding. "At Psomas Wines, of course," he says, gesturing with his food. "I've made some room for you at the top. With all of the work you've done at the hotel, I was thinking Vice President of Marketing would be a good fit. How does that sound?"

He thinks I'm planning to join Psomas Wines? He can't be serious. That is the furthest thing from reality I can imagine. I laugh. "That's not really what I was thinking."

"Okay," he says, undeterred. "Finance? Supply chain? We'll find something. That's the beauty of a family business—"

"No, Dad," I interrupt. "I don't want to work at Psomas Wines. I want to go back to the States."

The long moment that follows is filled solely with muffled conversations from the other side of the restaurant.

"What about starting a U.S. division of the company? Andres and I have always talked about expanding past Europe."

I take about fifteen seconds to consider his suggestion, but the idea sits in my stomach like a rock. A lifetime of butting heads with my dad over what his company should do sounds awful. "Dad, we've talked about this. I want to do my own thing. I don't want to be a part of the family business. That hasn't changed."

His face falls, happiness seeping from his eyes. "You're my only son, Niko. My only child. This is a family business."

My chest tightens. My father lowers his head and covers his brow with a hand. He took over this business from his dad and has grown it exponentially with his brother. He wants to pass that down. I understand, but just because I'm his only child doesn't mean I need to do that for him. My mom made the choices she did to raise me in California and show me a different path.

"I know, Dad," I finally tell him. "I am sorry, but I can't be that person for you. I wish I could. But my heart is not in it."

"You haven't even tried, son," he rebuts, placing both hands steadily on the table. "How do you know? How can you say that your heart isn't in a family business? This is our family. Our name. Your cousins. Me."

I take a deep breath. I was worried he would feel like I was abandoning him or the family. I have worked so hard to make a place for myself here. But it's just not enough for me. I know Dad feels like the business is family and there is no separation. That might be why he has always struggled to connect with me. He only knows how to communicate on a business level.

"Dad, living here has been a good experience. I have learned a great deal from you at the hotel and by watching you in the wine business. I still want to be part of the family even if I don't want to be a part of the business."

"I never should have let her take you to America. If I had kept you here, none of this would even be an issue."

That statement feels like a dagger straight to my stomach. It's as if he regrets my entire identity. He would rather I be someone else, someone who didn't know any different from this life, so that they wouldn't choose anything different.

I don't know what to say or where to even take the conversation from here.

Luckily, the waiter shows up with our entrées. We both thank him quietly and take a moment to settle into our meal. I cut my lamb into small pieces and push the potatoes around my plate. I have lost my appetite.

"Dad, I'm sorry, I don't want to hurt you, but—"

"No, Niko. I'm sorry. My comment was inappropriate."

My eyebrows shoot up. I can count on one hand the number of times my dad has apologized to me.

"Thank you. Like I said, I respect everything you have done with Psomas Wines. I want to find my own passion, something I believe in and can build from the ground up. Just like you did."

I expect him to push back. I expect him to tell me that he built the business for me, or that I can grow at Psomas Wines. But he doesn't. He takes a bite of his steak and chews.

"Do you understand?" I finally ask him, unable to take the silence anymore.

"My son," Dad says. "I don't understand, no. I wish you would follow in my footsteps so you don't have to work as hard as I did. I wish I could convince you. But you're right. We've had this conversation many times, and I don't want to argue."

He shrugs in resignation, but I'm relieved that he isn't fighting me, so I don't push it.

"Are you doing this for that girl? Is she the only reason you are making this decision?"

That girl.

He met Jenni. She presented to the board of directors. And he still refers to her as "that girl"? That tells me everything I need to know. He isn't going to change. He'll never understand that some relationships are more important than profit. But that's okay. Just because he is that way doesn't mean that I have to be.

"No," I tell him, honestly. "I thought about that a lot. I won't lie and tell you that being with her wasn't a factor in my decision. It was. She's affecting the timing more than anything else. I might have stayed longer if it weren't for her, but I don't think this was ever going to be my long-term path. Even if she broke up with me tomorrow, I still feel like it's time for me to move on from the Omorfiá. I have created a space that is meaningful and unique. It's time to redirect my efforts elsewhere. Hospitality has never been my dream job."

"No, you're a retail man, like myself," my dad responds. "Andres has always handled the hospitality arm of our business."

I hadn't ever thought about that, but it's true. Andres oversees all wine tastings and accommodations under Psomas

Wines. No wonder Ana has been incredible at the Omorfiá. But I'm more surprised that my dad sees something in me that resonates with him. It feels good.

"I'm proud of you, Niko," he continues. "When you first came here, I harbored secret hopes that you would step into the business, but I can respect wanting to pave your own way. I'll support your decision."

"You will?" I ask, knowing full well that I don't need his permission, but it would mean a lot to me.

"Yes," he says. "I'm not a perfect father, but I can see that this is what you want. I just hope you don't forget your family."

"I won't, Dad. Being back here has shown me how much I missed out on during my childhood. I want to continue building our relationship. Once I figure out what I'm going to do, I would love to have you as a mentor."

"Let's drink to that," he says, flagging down our waiter. "Can we get a round of ouzo?"

"Of course, sir," he says, disappearing toward the bar.

"Well, son, if you aren't going to be running the hotel I bought for you, I guess I'll be looking for a new general manager. When are you planning to leave?"

"I am leaving in a week for a Christmas vacation. If we can find someone to take over the hotel in the new year, I'd rather not come back."

He lets out a low chuckle. "That's not much time, Niko. You know how hard it is to find people this time of year."

"I do, but I have an idea about who can handle the job."

The waiter brings our ouzo, and my father grabs his glass. He raises it for a toast. "To new beginnings."

We clink glasses and each take a swig of our alcohol.

"Who is this mysterious person you'd like to take your place?" he asks.

I smile. This is going to be fun.

9

Jenni

The familiar sound of Catherine O'Hara screaming *"Kevin!"* in first class blares from my laptop, and Sarah laughs. "Honestly, I think I could watch this movie five hundred times and not get tired of it. But how does a mother forget her child?"

"I don't know," I say. "It was the early nineties, I get the feeling that childhood was like the wild west back then. Every kid for themselves."

"True. Can you hand me the glue gun?"

I pass the glue gun over to her across the plastic folding table we've set up in the lobby of the inn. Sarah and I are working on Christmas decorations for the inn—another way the girls are trying to save money. Who knew that Christmas decor was so expensive? Adulting is wild.

Sarah and I visited a bulk craft store in Denver a few weeks ago, and we've been slowly creating our own wreaths and ornaments. I'm tying giant bows out of velvet ribbon and attaching wire so that we can line the banister of the main staircase. The red and green plaid ribbon with gold metallic stitching looks like something that could have been in the McAlister household in Home Alone.

"How many wreaths is that?" I ask.

"Six, I think. Just four more. Unless we want to hang them in the hallways or around the downstairs areas." Sarah is gluing juniper berries to a faux evergreen wreath. She has piles of pine cones, holly berries, white and pink flocked pine branches, and ribbons in a variety of festive colors. We're going to hang one on each guest room door.

"Almost done," I tell her. "I think the Christmas trees and poinsettias are enough for downstairs. But maybe we can put ribbons on the artwork."

"Oh, maybe we could cut paper snowflakes for down here," Sarah suggests. "I saw the cutest thing online where someone used old newspapers and sewed all the snowflakes together into a garland."

"That would be perfect," I tell her. "I can grab my mom's sewing machine when I go feed the chickens this afternoon."

A few minutes and two more bows later, a can of paint swings down from Kevin's upstairs landing and knocks Harry over, so that he's lying on top of Marv.

"You know, this movie would be the ultimate rom-com if those two were falling in love," I remark. "Two accident-prone criminals, afraid to acknowledge their feelings for each other until a job goes so terribly wrong that they fear they'll lose each other?"

Sarah laughs and drops the wreath she's working on. "I think you've either been watching too many made-for-TV holiday movies or you're really missing Niko."

"Probably both," I admit. I have been binging cable Christmas movies while packing my apartment. I have two boxes in my car that I need to take to my parents' house later. The hard part is packing in such a way that no one notices. I haven't told anyone except Amber about my plans to head to Greece. The boxes are filled with random things I don't need right now, like summer clothes and office supplies. All the things no one will notice are gone if they stop by the apartment. I don't want anyone to realize my apartment is half empty. Not Niko. And definitely not the girls.

I wish I could tell Piper and Sarah, because I feel an obsessive need for reassurance that I'm not making a huge mistake. They've been so stressed with the opening of the inn, though, and I don't want to drop a bomb in their laps. I have to help them get this place up and running, and then I can tell them I'm leaving.

"Hey, are you okay?" Sarah asks. "You seem stuck in your head."

"Yeah, I'm fine. Just nervous about seeing Niko again. What if the magic is gone? What if we only work when I'm pretending to be the type of person who belongs at a Greek resort? He might not like small-town Jenni."

"I don't know, hon," Sarah says. "I think the two of you have spent enough time together that Niko knows the real you. Why else would he be coming out here for Christmas?"

"Because he's too nice to break things off over the phone? Because he made a promise at the end of a crazy week of sunshine and romance, and he's loyal to a fault?"

Sarah puts down the ribbon she's trimming for her last wreath. "I know this is a lot. Your relationship has been very unconventional, but I think most men wouldn't maintain a long-distance relationship like he has if they weren't invested. You can trust Niko."

I know she's right. On a logical level, it makes perfect sense that Niko wouldn't come here to spend Christmas with me if he wasn't interested in something long-term. Nobody travels six thousand miles for a booty call. However, so much of our story has felt too good to be true, and historically, I'm not the type of person whose life goes that way.

"I know, but I hate it. I wish I could know how things would be if we had a *conventional* relationship. I'm so over the phone calls and the distance and existing as a couple in scattered weeks spread out over months." I trim the ends of a bow into inverted points and fluff up the bunny ears. "I'm sorry. I shouldn't complain. I feel stuck."

The irony makes me laugh. I felt like this before I went to Greece and met Niko. Maybe I'm doomed to always feel as if I'm living in the in-between.

"It's perfectly understandable," Sarah says. "Just don't let it mess with you. You and Niko are great together. I already know that without having even met him. I'm sure you'll figure things out. It beats the alternative of not being together, right?"

The thought makes my insides turn cold. I'm afraid that we'll end this holiday season going our separate ways for good. I don't want to admit how much that idea haunts me. If Niko and I can't make this work, then what? How am I just supposed to move on?

"You're right, it definitely beats the alternative," I say, straightening up. "Thanks, Sarah. I'm going to hang these ribbons on the banister. Want to help?"

"Oh, yes! I can't wait to see them, it's going to feel so festive," she says, springing to her feet.

AFTER ADORNING the stairs with ribbon and hanging a few of the wreaths on the guest room doors, I make the drive to my parents' house, without any clarity on my Niko situation. I wish I could look into a crystal ball and know, for sure, that he is going to react with joy when I show him the airplane ticket.

My parents live on a windy road on the outskirts of town. Their house is nestled among the trees at the end of a long gravel driveway. It's not uncommon to see deer or even a red fox ambling about on their property. One of my favorite things to do growing up was to peer out my bedroom window in the early morning hours and watch the wildlife before the hustle and bustle of our family sent them scurrying away.

The yellow house is already adorned with Christmas lights, featuring fresh evergreen garland strung along the railing of the wrap-around porch. In the summer, wild flowers will pop up all around the property, but right now the area surrounding the house looks mostly brown and gray, except for the evergreens and a few patches of snow.

After dropping my boxes upstairs and grabbing my mom's egg apron, I make my way to the back of the house, where my dad built a chicken run over twenty years ago.

My parents have a flock of ten hens, and I take care of them when my parents are away. They don't require much work, just refreshing their food and water and collecting eggs every day. An automatic door on their coop shuts at night to protect them from predators, so I only have to come once a day.

"Hey, ladies," I say, as I undo the latch on the spring-loaded door of the run. "Glad to see everyone accounted for." I check the laying boxes and fill my apron pockets with fresh eggs.

"Good job, girls. We have a lot of eggs in here," I say, after pulling two more eggs out of the last lay box.

I sigh. If I can't talk to Sarah and Piper, maybe talking to the chickens will at least get some of my anxiety off my chest. "I'm starting to think I've put all my eggs in one basket with this long-term trip to Mykonos," I tell them.

The hens don't respond, other than clucking and waddling around looking for bugs in the cold ground.

"On the one hand," I say, as I move to check the water

dispenser. "How will I ever know what Niko and I could be if I don't take a chance on spending time together, right?"

At this point, Piper would chime in with some witty response or innuendo, but the chickens continue to go about their business, waiting for me to refill their grain dish.

"On the other hand, I am opening myself up for a world's worth of rejection if it doesn't go well."

After shaking all the gunk out of the water dispenser, I step outside the enclosure to refill the water basin. When I return, I stare at the chickens. "What do you think? Am I crazy for taking this risk?"

One of my favorite black and white speckled hens pecks at my boot. "Clearly, I have gone crazy if I'm asking chickens for advice on my love life."

I wish, for the hundredth time, that I could talk to Sarah and Piper about this. But the chickens are the only girlfriends I've got right now.

"Okay, fine. Cluck once for *way too risky* or twice for *you've met the love of your life, and that's worth the risk.*"

Silence. It's like the birds have gone mute.

"Great," I tell them. "Super helpful. Thank you."

I lift the lid on their grain box and refill it. As the grain rattles against the tin, all the hens come hopping, flapping, and running over in a chorus of squawks and clucks in the cool winter air. "Oh, now you have something to say? I see how it is."

I pick up one of the hens closest to me, stroking her soft feathers and down coat. "What's a girl going to do, huh?"

Just ask him, she seems to say as she side-eyes the pellets below.

Asking Niko will ruin everything. I really want it to be a surprise. Maybe I can gauge his interest without asking. There has to be a way to tell if he would balk at the idea of me moving to the Omorfiá. I could start making plans for a future trip and see what he says. It would only be fair to take turns visiting each other.

That could even be a good cover. We could plan an extravagant trip for March or April. I can make a big deal about counting down the days until the next time we'll be together, and then, on Christmas morning, I'll tell him it was all a ruse and I'm coming *now*.

That would work.

"Good idea, sweetie," I say to the hen and set her down. "I'll just have to trick him into reassuring me that he wants me in his life. That won't be too hard, right?"

I reach into my pocket and pull out a handful of apple slices and zucchini chunks to supplement the grain pellets, as a gesture of thanks for their help.

I head back to my car after locking everything up, feeling determined. All I have to do is talk to Niko about visiting him without specifying when or for how long. As long as he's excited about the idea, I can go through with my Christmas surprise. It's a foolproof plan.

10

Niko

I walk out to the front desk of the hotel. Our head concierge, Alexander, should be finishing up his shift soon, having just been joined by the temporary night concierge. Alexander is one of our most valuable employees, and as such, I want to get his take on something. He always has a read on both the staff and the guests and knows what everyone needs at any given moment. I want to catch him before his shift ends so that I don't keep him here any longer than he needs to stay.

"Alexander, if you're free. Can you join me in my office for a few minutes?"

He jumps. "Mr. Psomas! Yes, sir, I'm free. Yes."

I smile. He always sounds like he's nervous, but I know it's because he feels such a calling to make sure everyone at the hotel is taken care of. That's why he is such a great concierge.

"Perfect, come in."

Once we are both settled into chairs on opposite sides of my desk, I offer him a glass of water.

"Thank you, Mr. Psomas, but can I ask what this is regarding? Has something happened? Can I help you with anything?"

I smile. Something has happened, but I can't tell him what quite yet. "Alexander, you were here before my father bought the hotel and before I took over as general manager. Now that it's been almost a year, I was hoping you could tell me what you think."

"What I think, sir?"

"Yes. What do you think about the changes we've made, and how the staff is getting along?"

He sits up straighter, beaming. "It's all wonderful, Mr. Psomas. The hotel has come back to life. You've made changes for the better, and the staff loves working for you. No one wants to leave."

I can feel my shoulders relax. Even if Alexander has a slight tendency to exaggerate sometimes, I can only do this if I'm confident that everyone is taken care of and happy. As desperate as I am to go back to the States and make a commitment to Jenni, I don't want to jeopardize what I've built here. I can't abandon them. If they aren't ready, if my plan doesn't work quite yet, I can be patient.

"And Ana? Do you think she is prepared to run the place while I'm in Colorado for a few weeks?"

Alexander blushes. I don't know if it's because of the mention of Ana or the fact that I'm visiting Jenni. He adores both of them.

"Miss Ana is amazing, Mr. Psomas. Amazing."

Yep, I should have known his schoolboy crush on Ana hadn't simmered since she moved here full-time.

"Miss Ana will do a great job with the hotel; you don't need to worry at all. Not one bit."

That is true. "Do you think the staff respects her? Will they be happy to have her in charge while I'm gone?"

Alexander pauses. "Yes, Mr. Psomas, absolutely. Most of the staff credits Ana for being able to keep our jobs through the winter months. If you don't mind me saying so."

I laugh. He looks like he just divulged some secret. "I believe the same, Alexander. Ana is definitely keeping this place open through the tourism lull with all of her event planning."

I don't know if I can ask any more questions without letting on that bigger changes are coming, so instead I change the subject. "You know, I don't think I've asked. What do you have planned for the holidays, Alexander?"

"My brothers are coming home with their children. It's going to be a big Christmas morning with them around to take part in all the traditions! We'll make the Christmas bread, smash pomegranates, and decorate the family boat. We haven't done it in years."

I feel a tiny bit jealous. Since my mom raised me in California, I have never participated in Greek holiday traditions. I'm sad I'll miss it again, but not sad enough to stay. Maybe next year, Jenni and I can visit ... if she'll have me. As much as I know that I want to be with her, we haven't talked about our long-term future. I could be setting myself up for major disappointment with this move to the States. It's worth it, though. It's time for a change.

"That sounds great. I hope you have a wonderful time with your family. Send me pictures of the boat, okay?"

"Of course, sir. I will! Is that all?"

"Yes, but can you ask Ana to come in, please? She should be in her office."

Alexander exits, and I'm alone in my quiet office. This is it. I can't go back after this. Dad already told me that if I change my mind, I can stay as general manager. Once I have this conversation, however, I'm no longer the only person affected.

I would never make an offer to Ana or anyone else and then retract it. This decision must be final. I pause, checking in with my body. There's a lightness in my chest, and a tingling sensation buzzing just beneath the surface. I'm excited about this new step in my life, which is enough to propel me forward. I know it's the right decision, regardless of what happens in Colorado.

"Knock, knock." My cousin stands in the doorway, a gracious smile on her face. "You needed to talk?"

"Yes, take a seat."

She does, crossing her legs. She's wearing a white business suit with gold-colored heels. Ana always looks put together and classy. Having grown up in the Greek hospitality industry, she's perfect for this role in a way that I could never be.

"I have something important to ask you."

"Okay ... sounds ominous." She giggles.

I am not starting on the right foot. I want her to be excited, not anxious.

"No, it shouldn't. It's good news. I had dinner with Dad a few nights ago, and we talked about the future of the hotel."

Outrage creeps across Ana's face, her features turning sharp as her lips purse. "Don't tell me he is thinking about selling it now that we've turned it around. That's so typical. No investment of the heart. Just money, money, money with those two."

She's referring to Dad and Andres.

"No, no." I put my hands up, signaling to her that it's okay. "Nothing like that."

She huffs. "Then what crazy idea have they come up with now?"

I'm tempted to rile her up. I love her fiery streak. But I

don't want to distract us from the important offer I am about to present.

"Actually, I'm the one with the idea, and I don't think it's crazy at all." I smile at her as her brows knit in confusion. "I would like to hire you as my replacement. I think you should be the general manager of the Omorfiá Hotel."

Ana's jaw drops, and she stares at me.

I expect her to say something, but a moment passes, and she still looks like she's processing what I said. "Hello? Earth to Ana."

"Niko!" she shouts. "What are you talking about? *Me?* I can't be the general manager. For a few weeks, maybe, but not permanently. Why? Aren't coming back?"

I smile.

"Oh, my gosh. Are you not coming back? Are you moving back to California?"

I say nothing.

"Colorado?" Ana's eyes widen as she puts the pieces together. "Are you moving there to be with Jenni?" She squeals and stands up, towering over the desk. "This is the best news ever! Tell me everything. What did she say when you told her? Did she die from happiness?"

"I haven't told her yet, actually," I say. I have debated so many times, but I want to tell her in person. I want to tell her on Christmas morning. Saying it over the phone when we only get four minutes to talk doesn't feel right. "I want it to be a surprise on Christmas Day. Do you think she'll be happy?"

Ana looks like she might burst into tears. "That is the most romantic thing I've ever heard! Niko, she's going to be thrilled. She misses you so much." Ana comes around the desk and pulls me up. "Oh, I'm just so happy for you!"

I embrace her. She knows how important Jenni is to me, and it feels great to have her support.

"Does that mean you'll take the job?"

"Oh." Ana's face fills with fear as her eyes widen. "I forgot about that part."

"Please? It's the only way I'll feel good about leaving. I need to know that the hotel will be in capable hands."

Ana holds up two perfectly manicured hands. "These hands? Niko, these hands are not capable."

I laugh. "Of course, they are. You practically run the place already. You said so yourself. The staff respects you. I already talked to my dad, and he agrees that you are perfect. You were made for this job, Ana."

"He really said that?" Ana looks like she might cry.

"He did. The job is yours if you want it. Oh, and I'll be joining the board to keep both of our fathers in check."

She guffaws. "Oh, please. I can handle them."

I smile. That's the version of Ana I know and love. Once she gets the hang of it, she'll have our fathers eating out of the palm of her hand.

"When will this start?"

"Depending on how things go in Colorado, I won't be coming back after Christmas. But either way, Ana, this isn't the job for me. I've realized that while watching you. You have the passion and drive for hospitality. I've been following your lead for months. I need to find something else for myself."

Now, she is crying. I hand her a tissue. "I'll miss you. It's been so amazing having you here, working together."

"I'll miss you, too. But Jenni and I will visit all the time. Don't worry. You'll get sick of us."

She makes eye contact with me, balling the tissue in her hand. "Okay."

"Okay, you'll get sick of us? Or okay you'll—"

"I'll take the job!"

She jumps into another hug and squeezes me tight. Relief washes through my body. This was the right move. It's going to make everyone happy.

"So, you really think Jenni will be excited?" I finally ask after she lets me go.

"Niko, stop acting like a nervous little boy. If this is something you want to do, just do it. Have the courage, regardless of how she might react. What are you afraid of?"

I don't know how to answer that question.

I guess I'm worried that if Jenni is experiencing success in her life and feeling more confident and capable, I might not fit into it. She might not need me now that she is so happy in her own life. She doesn't need me to lift her anymore. I want her to thrive and live her life to the fullest. I just hope there is a place for me alongside her.

"Nothing," I tell Ana. Even though I consider her a sister, I can't voice that vulnerability. I need to put up a brave face for her as she embarks on her new career at the hotel. "It's just a pretty big gesture, and sometimes I can go overboard."

"You mean, like when you spent weeks hiding ducks around the hotel just to set up a surprise party? Trust me, Jenni knows you go overboard. You don't have anything to worry about. She loves a grand gesture."

"You're right," I tell her. "Well, I think we need to celebrate your promotion." I retrieve a bottle of wine from the mini fridge next to my desk and two glasses from a shelf on the wall.

After pouring the wine, I hold out a glass to Ana.

"To new beginnings," I toast.

"To getting the girl," Ana adds, before taking a sip of her wine.

As the alcohol hits my bloodstream, a tenuous buzz of excitement courses through me. With all of the pieces in place, there's just one more thing to do. Tomorrow, I will plan the best Christmas surprise reveal of all time. And then in a week, I'll fly to Colorado with my entire life in a suitcase.

11

Piper

I drop the tailgate of the used pickup truck I bought when we decided to settle in Pineview Springs. The hinges scream with age, dirt, and grime. I add WD-40 to the long mental list of things I need to do. I'll take care of it in a few weeks, as soon as I fix the industrial stove at the inn, find replacement bedding, finish the landscaping, and winterize this RV.

We're fortunate that we've been able to store it in a garage at Sarah's parents' house; otherwise, we might have suffered damage from the early storms when the temperatures dropped below freezing. But I've reached my level of comfort in relying on her parents' generosity and want to give Sarah's dad his workspace back. I'm just grateful they're letting us keep it on their property, parked next to the garage.

"Okay, where should I start?" Jenni says, grabbing a bucket filled with rags and cleaning supplies.

"Let's give it a good clean inside." I haul down the air compressor and set it outside the RV. "Then I'll blow out the pipes and water tank."

I unlock the door and climb into the RV. The warm, earthy scent of yellowing vinyl and laminate surfaces coated in dust from across the United States hits me. It smells like home, and memories of Sarah and me traversing the country in this RV pop up from every nook and cranny. After college, neither of us wanted to settle down, so we both took remote jobs and went to all the places we had dreamed of while growing up in the mountains. I didn't realize how much I've missed that togetherness and freedom since we moved into the inn full-time.

"Wow, it's stale in here," Jenni says, and I startle, forgetting she was right behind me. Her impression is so different from mine, but I guess it would be. She didn't find herself within these mobile walls. I did.

"Something like that. Here." I toss her a linen grocery bag.

Jenni gets to work emptying the cupboards of cans and dry goods while I spray down the counters. We've been so busy that we never gave this place a move-out clean, and it shows. I think part of me has wanted to keep it as a getaway car. If the town turns on us, or things don't work out, we could get out of here, away from any problems, and go back to RV life.

After a few minutes, Jenni sets her bag down by the door and grabs a tub of disinfectant wipes before kneeling down in the bathroom.

"You don't need to do that," I say, moving toward her. "I can do the dirty work."

"Are you afraid of what I might find?" Jenni laughs. "We've been friends forever. I do not mind cleaning your toilet. It can't be worse than that time a guest got food poisoning at the inn, and you were the only maid on site to handle it. Remember?"

The memory makes me smile. It was so disgusting, but

sixteen-year-old Jenni offered to don gloves and a mask and get down and get dirty with me so I didn't have to do it alone. She's that kind of friend.

"Okay." I give in. "Make my life easier, if you have to."

I have missed this easy banter. Being on the road was amazing, but being home, with Sarah and Jenni all living in one place, is what dreams are made of. I'm glad she decided to stay in Pineview Springs after receiving her promotion. I don't think I'd be able to do this without her.

"Have you girls thought about selling this thing now that you are settled?" Jenni asks from the bathroom. "I bet you could get decent money for it."

Money has been so tight that I have thought about it. I won't bring that up to Sarah, however. The RV is her baby. Every detail in this thing, from the cupboards painted to look like a sunset to the hand-embroidered curtains, is a piece of her. And it represents our life, our commitment to each other. She is way too sentimental to let it go.

"No, not really. It's in Sarah's name because I had more student debt when we bought it. So, I guess that's her call."

I try to sound casual, as if it isn't something that's weighing on me. We could solve so many problems by selling the RV, but I can't break Sarah's heart like that. I am already stifling her dreams nearly every day with the inn. I can't take this away as well.

Jenni laughs. "Then you can guarantee you won't be selling it any time soon. She loves this thing."

If anyone else said something like that about my girlfriend, I would roll up my sleeves and take them outside. But Jenni loves Sarah as much as I do. I know she says it without judgment. "Yep, there's a reason I haven't bought it up."

We settle into silence as I take out the handheld vacuum and get all the crumbs and cobwebs in the nooks and crannies. Jenni takes the sheets off the bed and puts all the linens into a laundry bag so we can take them home, wash them, and store them. The place is finally cleaned out from our life on the road. And it feels like a door shutting on that part of our life.

"I'm going to go disconnect the water tank and heater. Can you open the faucets and flush the toilet before meeting me outside?"

I step out of the RV and onto the gravel of Sarah's parents' driveway. It crunches beneath my boots. Closing up the RV is hitting me harder than I thought it would. I'm sure someday we'll take it camping or on a road trip if we can ever leave the inn for an extended time, but it won't ever be the same.

I crawl partway under the vehicle to undo the latch on the tank drain and disconnect the water heater. My breath catches as water pours out onto the gravel as I extricate myself from the undercarriage. It finally feels real. As the water creates a small pool on the driveway, I hear Jenni's tennis shoes crunch the gravel behind me. I wipe my eyes before standing to meet her gaze.

Jenni sets down the bucket of cleaning supplies. "You know, it's sad to see it just sit here. I know that's what most RVs do in the winter, but I never thought I'd see the day when you retired it."

Me neither. I knew we would settle down eventually, but I didn't expect it to happen so soon.

"She really is meant to be out there exploring, isn't she?" I remark. We decided a long time ago that the RV was female, but we never got around to naming her.

"If Sarah were here, she'd have some brilliant idea for its next stage of life. We should call her."

The water dripping out of the RV subsides to a few drops. Jenni's right. Sarah would probably suggest that we turn the RV into an extra guest room at the inn. Or perhaps turn it into an on-site art studio. I can see the way her eyes would sparkle with the idea.

Until I shut it down and ruin the moment, like I always do.

However, Jenni's words from the other day have been stuck in my head.

"Sarah wants someone to dream with her."

I shouldn't jump to conclusions about why something won't work. If I were to dream alongside her, I would be trying to come up with a creative way to use the RV, rather than saying it has to be put out to pasture just because we're settling down.

And then, like a three-ton vehicle falling from the sky, it hits me.

A smile the size of Texas crosses my face as I hook the air compressor to the tank. Jenni, who is returning from the garage with an extension cord for the compressor, stops in her tracks. "What's that smile on your face for?"

"I'll tell you when we're done. This thing is loud." I need to flesh this idea out for a minute and make sure it has legs before I get anyone excited.

Jenni covers her ears, and I turn on the compressor, which sends the last drops of water shooting out of the drain. Now nothing should freeze and crack the pipes during the cold months.

However, that might not be a concern if my idea comes to fruition. Maybe the RV doesn't have to sit here all winter. I can kill two birds with one stone. Make Sarah's dreams come true and keep the RV in our lives.

I turn off the compressor and toss Jenni a towel. "Do you remember when Sarah mentioned wanting a bookstore at the inn? Do you think she was serious?" I ask, as we head back inside to wipe up any water from the faucets.

Jenni considers for a moment. "I don't see why she wouldn't be. She always has a book with her. I bet she'd love it."

I wipe down the kitchen sink, trying to gain the courage to share my idea. I shouldn't be nervous; this is Jenni. However, suggesting something this creative is way outside my comfort zone, and I don't know how she'll react. She might not even believe that it's a real idea.

"If we turned these cabinets into shelves and took out the bed, how many books do you think we could fit in here?" I ask.

Jenni's eyebrows knit together as she processes my question. Then her eyes go wide and she squeals. "Are you asking what I think you're asking?"

"I guess that depends. Do you think I'm asking whether or not I can turn this RV into a bookstore for Sarah?"

Jenni jumps up and down, knocking her shoulder on one of the painted cupboard doors. "Ouch," she cries, before wrapping me up in a hug. "Piper Morris, I knew you were capable of dreaming. It's going to be amazing, and Sarah is going to die. Where do we start?"

That is a good question. I don't know. I should have thought this through. "I guess by getting another business license? Finding a wholesaler?"

Jenni sighs. "The anti-romantic is back. Piper, you do not start with paperwork. Sarah isn't going to care about that. Start with a name. Build a sign. Make the grand gesture. You can figure out the details later."

Oh. I guess that is the more romantic gesture. I think about it for a moment. I can build a sign, and I already know the name. "It's a good thing we got the RV out of Stan's garage. I'm going to need his table saw for that sign. Let's stop inside before we leave and see if he has any lumber I can use."

Jenni lights up, clapping her hands. "Yes! Oh, my gosh. This is going to be perfect!"

Fingers crossed, she's right. As I picture the type of sign I could build, my heart flutters at the thought of Sarah's surprised face when I show her. She will never expect it.

12

Sarah

GOLDEN, COLORADO
EARLY DECEMBER

A small bell chimes when I open the glass door to the pawn shop, setting my nerves on edge. The shop is empty except for the tattooed man with long white hair, a huge white beard, and a red bandana tied around his forehead. *Great.* Just the type of person who will want to help me get an engagement ring for my girlfriend. He looks like someone who would call our relationship a lifestyle choice.

"What can I do for you, miss?"

I have racked my brain trying to come up with a way to make some money for the mall store ring without any success. With some luck, maybe I'll find a ring that catches my eye. But not with this biker gang man hovering over my shoulder.

I brush him off. "I'm just going to look at some jewelry. Nothing in particular."

He smiles and gestures with one of his burly hands toward

the far end of the store. "It's in those cases. When you see something you want, just let me know and I'll unlock it for you."

He goes back to whatever magazine he had been reading when I came in. Hopefully, he'll let me browse in peace. As I approach the cases, my stomach turns. Part of me hopes I find a ring that works, but the rest of me wants to run as fast as I can out of here. I don't feel comfortable, and I don't expect anything I find to be good enough for Piper.

It was silly even to stop the car and walk through the door. I came down to Golden to pick up a few tools that Piper put on hold at a home improvement store, but then I saw the signs for the pawn shop, and it was as if I lost all control of my body and found myself swerving off the highway toward the store. Perhaps that ring in Denver isn't the end-all, be-all I believe it is. Maybe another ring will evoke the same feelings. Proposing to Piper is more important than having the perfect ring. It shouldn't matter what I use.

I reach the jewelry cabinets. Exotic-looking necklaces covered in rubies, emeralds, and pearls fill the middle shelf in a mosaic of color. All shapes and sizes. It's like a gem-studded chocolate box, each piece offering something different.

Each case of jewelry must hold a hundred stories: desperate mothers trying to pay the rent, jilted lovers tossing the last reminders of a failed relationship, grandchildren who have lost sight of sentimentality, or theft and deceit.

"How do you verify the jewelry for authenticity and ownership?" I call back to the man at the register, feeling guilty by association at the thought of any of these pieces having tragic backstories.

He saunters over. "I've gotten pretty good at recognizing a fake over the years. But I have a jeweler I can call if I need help. If it's a diamond, we require the certificate to prove ownership. If it's antique or another type of jewelry, we do our best. It's not a perfect system, but we haven't had too many problems."

It's a more thoughtful answer than I expected. I wouldn't have been surprised if he said he didn't care about ownership at all. But everything I know about pawn shops comes from what I've seen in movies, where they are portrayed as seedy and don't keep records, so the police can't implicate them.

"Not looking for anything in particular, you said?" the man asks with a twinkle in his eye and a rosy tint to his cheeks. "Usually when someone comes into the shop for jewelry, it's because they know what they want, but just can't afford it."

I meet his eyes. Kindness laces his smile. He feels safe.

"You caught me. I'm actually looking for an engagement ring. Are these the only ones you have?" I gesture toward the top shelf in the glass cabinet.

"Yep, that's it. Are you shopping for a man or a woman?"

I look up in surprise. I didn't expect that sort of question from him.

"My granddaughter has a girlfriend. She's been helping me learn gaydar. I saw the pink and orange flag pin on your bag strap."

Tension seeps from my body, my neck and chest loosening. That was … a pleasant surprise.

"I'm shopping for my girlfriend. But she's pretty masculine, so a man's ring would probably work best. She'd never wear a typical diamond engagement ring."

He opens the back of the cabinet and pulls out the tray of men's rings. Cobalt. Tungsten. There's a braided silver band that catches my eye, but it's way too big for Piper. My

"Let's take a look at the women's rings," he says. "If not the engagement rings, some of the bands might work."

He sets the men's tray back in the cabinet and replaces it with a red velvet tray holding diamond engagement rings and their matching bands. The Victorian-style ornate rings are an immediate hard pass. The simple rings featuring rows of rubies or floral engravings are better, but don't scream Piper. None of them takes my breath away like the first one at the mall.

I pick up a simple gold band with detailed engraving around the edges. It's the right size, but something about it feels wrong. It looks like a ring my mom might wear. It doesn't have the edgy flair that Piper carries, that she deserves.

I slump down to my elbows on the glass counter.

"Not going to work?"

"No, I'm sorry," I tell the pawn man. "It's not your fault. I saw this amazing ring at a shop in Denver a few weeks ago, but I can't afford it. I can't get it out of my head, either. It's perfect for her. Nothing else compares."

He runs his hand over his beard.

"Well, you know, we also buy goods. You got anything to sell? You could make some money for that ring."

His expression is so earnest that I can tell he wants to help. He's not just trying to grift me.

"Unfortunately, not. We've recently settled down after spending the past few years living in an RV, so I barely have any possessions to my name. Money is pretty tight."

"If you're settling down, do you need that RV anymore?"

My chest tightens. The RV? I couldn't. It's our baby. Our sweat, blood, and tears have gone into that thing.

But that perfect ring.

"Do you buy RVs?" I ask, tentatively.

He laughs. "No, no. I don't have the space or know-how for that. But you could sell it online. There are marketplaces for that type of thing. I would guess the supply is low this time of year. It'll go fast at the right price."

I wring my hands as I think it over. What would Piper say?

She'd probably be happy I made the right financial decision for once. We would have money left over after buying the ring that could help with cash flow at the inn, which has to count for something.

"Thank you so much," I tell him, "for your help and ideas."

"Happy holidays," he responds. "And once your girl says 'yes,' you should come back here and find a ring for yourself, okay?"

A ring for myself? I hadn't even considered that. "I will!"

My head is spinning with possibilities as I rush to the car. Once seated in the driver's seat, I pull out my phone to search RV marketplaces.

I find a handful, and before I know it, I'm uploading the pictures Piper sent me earlier of the winterized RV and writing a basic description of the make, model, and mileage. Before I can second-guess myself, I post it. The worst that can happen is that a few people are interested, and I decline their offer. Nothing requires me to sell it to the first person who clicks on my listing.

I scroll through the site, curious about what else is on the market, when my phone vibrates, catching me so off guard, I drop it to the floorboard. When I retrieve the phone, there's a text from Piper.

> Piper: Hey! How's it going? Did you get the tools?

> Sarah: Yes, I did. I'm almost headed back. I saw an antique shop I wanted to check out. Heading to the car now, though. And don't worry, I didn't buy anything.

I hate lying to her, but this is one secret I don't feel bad about keeping.

Piper: Sounds good. I'm almost done building the shelves for the dining room. Your dad has been a huge help. With those tools, I'll be able to install them at the inn tonight.

I didn't realize my dad was helping her. I thought all she had to do was sand some planks and attach brackets. I didn't think she'd need help with that. My dad probably just wanted to feel useful, and she included him.

Sarah: Give him a hug for me! See you soon.

I love that they are spending time together. It feels like a little glimpse of the future—my whole family, together for the holidays.

I close out of my messages and copy my listing to a few other sites. If I can sell the RV before Christmas Eve, it could be the miracle I've been waiting for.

13

Piper

As I sweep the broken tile into a dustbin, I wonder if I should be concerned about how much I enjoyed demolishing the bathroom floor. Honestly, taking a sledgehammer to the tile and watching it smash into pieces at my feet was cathartic. The raw power and force of it helped me feel in control when everything outside this bathroom feels like it's going a hundred miles an hour.

There are so many moving parts involved with getting the inn ready to open, and so many unknowns in the community. I need to fix the strain in my relationship with Sarah. At least I started working on a sign for the bookshop yesterday. Sarah's dad helped me draw up plans and cut all of the pieces.

"Hey," Sarah says, poking her head in from the hallway. "Are you ready for the mortar?"

I wipe the sweat from my brow. "Yeah, let's do it."

Sarah lugs in a five-gallon bucket, a bag of dry mortar, and a Bluetooth speaker from down the hall.

"What's the speaker for?" I ask.

"For mood music, obviously," Sarah says with a smile, and pulls out her phone and scrolls. In a few seconds, "Frosty the Snowman" echoes in the bathroom, and Sarah starts singing and shaking her hips.

I admire her before pulling her close, kicking up dust on the bare subfloor. How could anyone be mad at us for reopening the inn when Sarah's intentions are so pure and full of joy?

"You're the best," I tell her. "I am so glad I'm doing this with you."

"Tiling the bathroom? I'm sure Jenni or my dad would be way more helpful," she says, laughing.

"But they wouldn't be nearly as much fun," I tell her and pull her in for a kiss. "Nor would I want to kiss them."

The song changes to "Rockin' Around the Christmas Tree." I take a page out of Sarah's book and start dancing around the bathroom. She erupts in fits of giggles. "Yes, queen!" Sarah calls, joining me. We dance and sing and steal kisses while the song plays, and then stumble into the hallway.

"Why is it so hot in there?" Sarah gasps.

"Small confined space and clothing that is way too warm for dancing around?"

"Valid point," she says, fanning herself.

We mix the mortar in a bucket, and I use a notched trowel to spread it across the floor, starting in the back corner. It has the consistency of thick peanut butter and spreads easily on the floor. Once I have a small area covered, Sarah hands me individual tiles to place.

We picked are basic white subway tiles. The tile guy I talked to assured us that they would be a lot easier to match and replace if a tile ever breaks. Sarah convinced me to get navy accent tiles that we'll spread throughout.

"No, don't put that one there," Sarah says over my shoulder after I set down a white tile. "I want a blue one there."

I'm not surprised that she has strong opinions about where the accent tiles are going. I wouldn't have expected anything less. "Okay, blue it is. And then you want a white one here?" I ask, pointing to the next space.

"Exactly, you're brilliant," Sarah says, trying to appease me.

I pull up the tile, and it squelches, making Sarah laugh.

"Excuse you," she says, mocking disgust on her face.

"Oh, yes, that was definitely me, my bad," I say, and stick my tongue out at her.

"Do you remember when we bought the RV and decided to reupholster the couch? I made you redo it six times until it was perfect?"

"I had completely forgotten about that," I tell her. "But yes, you thought the pattern was crooked. I didn't think it mattered, but in the end, you were right. Once we got it perfect, I could tell the difference immediately."

"Just remember that I ended up being right for the next couple of hours, okay?" She gives me a sheepish grin.

"My love, I know you. This is not the last tile I'm going to need to rearrange."

Sarah has a relentless desire for perfection. She will fiddle with something for hours until it's exactly right. Usually, it pays off. It's why she is such a great artist. Whereas I rush through and get the job done and try not to worry about imperfections. It's one of the many ways that we balance each other out.

"As long as you know what you're getting yourself into," she says, tossing me the box of plastic spacers to slip in between the tiles.

"Have you thought at all about what we should do with the RV?" Sarah asks.

"The RV?" I respond, trying not to sound like I have something to hide. "No, I hadn't thought about it. I figure we'll keep it winterized and stored until we have more time to decide."

"You don't think we should sell it now?" She sounds casual, but there's a question in her eyes that tells me she's really trying to figure out what I want. The Sarah I know would never want to let go of something so incredibly sentimental to our relationship.

"No, I don't think there's any rush," I tell her. "Maybe eventually, but the RV is part of us. I don't want to get rid of such an important part of our identity."

"Oh, I assumed you would want to sell it." She looks taken aback, and a dull throng of guilt grows in my throat. Does she really think I would force her to get rid of such a special part of our history? Am I that hard on her about money?

I gesture for another tile and lay it down, wiggling it into place to ensure complete contact with the mortar. "I don't think we should make any decisions right away," I finally say. "I love the RV and all of the memories it holds. We'll figure out what to do with it eventually."

"Oh, okay," she says quietly, and then changes the subject back to the tiles in her hands. "Here, let's do another blue one there."

She hands me the tile, and I place it, using the plastic spacers to get it just right. When I turn back to Sarah, her eyes are unfocused, a distant look drawn on her face. "Are you okay?"

She shakes her head and snaps back to the present. "Yeah, definitely. Just imagining how amazing it's going to be once we get this bathroom done. Should we do a few of the other bathrooms, too?"

Before I can stop myself, I groan. I don't want to tile

another bathroom. Sarah reaches out and tickles my side. "I was kidding," she says.

"Don't scare me like that," I tell her, relief washing over me. "Do you want me to have a heart attack?"

"Never." She takes my hand and squeezes it. "Who would put gas in my car when I'm on empty?"

I bark out a laugh, but she keeps going.

"Who would get me coffee when I don't want to put pants on? Who would remember when the air conditioner needs maintenance?"

"I'm so glad you appreciate my contributions to the relationship," I tease.

"I love you," she says with a smile.

"I love you, too," I tell her. "Even if you give me heart attacks."

We work on the bathroom floor for a few more hours, interspersed with dance breaks. We sing and laugh, and it feels normal. It feels like we can forget about the stress and endless to-do lists and just be ourselves.

We don't talk about the RV again. Hopefully, I've convinced her that I am more than willing to hang onto it. I hate that she was worried I would make her sell it. I really need to do a better job at meeting her in the middle and showing her that I value her opinions and ideas.

"It looks great, Piper," Sarah says, admiring the floor. "You did such a good job."

"Thanks, it was fun," I tell her. "Want to help me grout it tomorrow after the mortar dries?"

She bats her eyes at me. "I thought you'd never ask."

14

Jenni

The airport is alive with Christmas spirit. An old-timey Christmas song plays over the speakers, and candy canes and snowflakes decorate the walls. There's even an ice skating rink at the outdoor plaza between the concourse and the airport hotel. This airport is primed for holiday cheer.

Thousands of people are traveling for the holidays. Families are heading on vacation, college students are coming home, and elderly grandparents are braving the crowds to see their grandchildren.

Even though the board says his plane landed thirty minutes ago, I haven't seen Niko.

My hands sweat, ruining the sign I'm holding that reads "Greek God." It's an inside joke from my first impressions of him on the island. The more weird looks I get, though, the more I'm starting to doubt using it.

I check my watch for the 100th time. Am I even in the right place? I think this is the exit he'll come out from off an international flight, but could I be wrong.

I have to ask someone. I can't just stand here with shaking hands and a racing heart that skips a beat every time I see a head of dark hair. I fold the paper sign and put it in my pocket before turning around to locate an information booth.

"Hey, you aren't leaving without me, are you?"

My entire body warms. I would recognize that voice anywhere. Hearing it in person takes me immediately back to the first time we met. He startled me from behind then, too, and I nearly toppled over, spilling an entire cup of pens across his lobby floor.

This time, I leap into Niko's arms and wrap mine around his neck. "You're here!"

"I'm here."

He picks me up and spins me around. I feel like I'm starring in every cheesy Christmas movie on television, but I don't care. Niko is here. He's really here.

Niko sets me down, but instead of grabbing his carry-on, which is now a few feet behind him, he grabs my waist and pulls me in for a kiss.

His warm lips meet mine, and I'm transfixed. I pull him closer, not wanting to let go or move. He pulls away, sliding his hands up my back and dipping me gently for another kiss. He breathes deeply as he presses his lips to mine again. The kiss is both gentle and firm, chaste and full of promise. I breathe him in.

It's amazing how even after a cross-Atlantic flight, he still smells and tastes like the ocean. Sea salt and pine. I've been trying to recreate that smell with candles, but nothing comes close to the real thing.

He straightens, pulling me up so I can regain my balance.

My lips tingle, feeling energized from the kiss, but my mind is clear. The world is right.

"Were you waiting long?" he asks.

"I, well … yes. But only because I arrived incredibly early. You know me."

"A chronic worrier who thinks she's late if she isn't five minutes early? Yes, I do." He wraps his hand around mine and squeezes it. "It's just the way I like you."

My cheeks flush. I tell myself it's because it's so warm in here, but deep down I know it's because I'm swooning like a schoolgirl.

Niko and I grab his suitcases from baggage claim.

"One of these is filled with things for my mom," Niko says, looking slightly embarrassed as he pulls his third suitcase off the conveyor belt. "She wanted me to bring half the island home to her."

We are visiting his mom in California after the holidays, and I can't wait.

"I don't blame her," I tell him. "If I thought you could bring me some loukoumades without them going stale, I would have requested a suitcase full as well."

"I actually have some in my back pocket, if you want to check."

I give him a confused look until I realize he's messing with me. I smile. I have missed his sense of humor. I feel silly for worrying so much about this visit.

A FEW HOURS LATER, we're alone in my apartment. On the one hand, I'm embarrassed about how small it is, or the lack of cohesive furniture and decor. On the other hand, I know Niko won't judge it because he knows just how much this place means to me.

"I love your view," he says, surveying the street below my kitchen window. "Pineview Springs is so cute."

I walk up next to him and lay my head on his shoulder in an embrace. "It really is. I don't know why I tried running from this place for so long."

He places a kiss on my forehead. "If you hadn't been trying to run, you might never have ended up at the Omorfiá, so I'm not complaining."

I reach up to kiss him, letting my body melt into his. I very much regret telling the girls we would meet them for dinner so they could meet Niko. I want him all to myself right now.

"What time are we meeting Piper and Sarah?" he asks, as if he read my mind.

"In twenty minutes," I respond, my tone forced. "But we could always cancel—"

"Absolutely not," he says, pulling away from me. "What sort of impression would that give your two best friends? I have been waiting months to meet them. I won't start by standing them up."

Why does he always have to be such a gentleman?

"Fine, but if you are tired or jet-lagged, just say the word, and we'll leave. Okay?"

"Deal. I'll tickle you under the table when I'm ready to leave."

I give him a stern look of disapproval. "You better not. I am too ticklish. I'll probably kick the table and send all the food flying." I can picture it now. It wouldn't be the first time I made a fool of myself in front of him.

"I guess I'd better not get tired then." He smiles, mischief in his eyes.

"Niko, please," I beg. "I don't think you understand. I will make a scene."

He shrugs and pulls me close. Before I can argue, we're

kissing again. If I'm not careful, we might not make it to dinner at all, so I push him away.

"Let's walk to dinner to wake you up and avoid the need for any under-the-table activity."

As we stroll along the dimly lit sidewalk, we can see our breath in the cool night air. It feels surreal that we're finally here, together. I smile at everyone we pass until we run into Charlie LeGrande. We pass by the old man outside a bar where he's smoking. Piper told me about their run-in at the hardware store when we were cleaning out the RV. I told her not to worry about him. His bark is way worse than his bite these days, and most people ignore him.

"Hi, Charlie," I say as we approach, not letting him dampen my mood. He looks Niko up and down before stomping out his cigarette.

"Hi, I'm Niko," he says, extending a hand to Charlie, who refuses to take it.

"Where are you from, Niko?" Charlie growls.

"California by way of Greece," Niko responds. He has placed his arm around me now that we have stopped to chat.

"Of course you are," Charlie says, disdain dripping from his words. "I hope you're not planning to move here. We have enough Californians already—"

"Nope, he's just visiting," I interrupt before Charlie can say anything else. I know where this is going, and we don't need it. Niko gives me a strained look. I continue, "We're actually late for dinner, Charlie. Have a good night."

When we're out of earshot, Niko asks, "Who was that?"

"No one," I say, rolling my eyes. "Just an old man who has been giving Piper a hard time about the inn."

"He doesn't seem to like outsiders," Niko observes.

"It's a good thing you are only visiting, or we might have had him chasing us out of town," I tell him.

"Yeah, I guess so," Niko says. His voice is quiet. He's already tired.

"Come on, perk up, we're almost there," I say, squeezing his hand.

When we reach the restaurant, Piper and Sarah are already here, looking warm and toasty in their winter best. They rarely ever beat me somewhere, but when they do, it's because they already have a whole plan of how the evening is going to go. They probably have a printed list of questions for Niko. I should have warned him.

"You must be Niko," Sarah says, her voice shrill and squeaky. She wraps Niko in a hug before he can respond.

"It's so great to meet you finally," Piper tells him. "Jenni has been a different person since you met."

"We take credit for that, by the way," Sarah interrupts. Oh boy, they're already bombarding him. "It was at this very restaurant that we convinced her to go and told her you were hot."

Niko gives me a quizzical look. "I think I need to hear this story," he says.

"No, you don't." I don't dare tell him the girls had a twenty-dollar bet on if we would hook up. Some pre-relation-ship details are best left unshared. "Let's grab our table. I'm starving."

Niko puts his hand on my back as we make our way through the restaurant, leaning down to whisper in my ear.

"You never told me you thought I was hot before we met," he says.

"Oh, my gosh. Stop," I say, my cheeks turning crimson. "Sarah said that, not me. I didn't think you were my type, actually."

"Because I was too good-looking?"

"Because you seemed arrogant."

Niko erupts in laughter, and a few heads turn our way. Surprisingly, I don't care. This sort of attention used to make me want to hide. Now, it doesn't worry me. Let them look. I'm with the people who make me happy.

After we take our seats, Niko opens the menu, then closes it, and turns to me. "I think it's your turn to tell me what to eat, actually."

I still dream of all the food Niko and I ate during my two weeks in Greece. "I don't know if we have anything as exciting as Greek pastries, but you're in the right place for a Colorado specialty. I can order for you if you want."

"Let's do it," he says. I love that he'll try anything. This must have been what it felt like for him when I was at the Omorfiá. When the waitress comes to take our order, I request two bowls of old-fashioned green chili for each of us. It's a Colorado staple, especially during the winter.

"The green chilis are grown in Pueblo, Colorado," I tell him. "And even though New Mexico will fight us over this, our chilis are the best in the world. They are roasted to perfection and then stewed with pork, masa, onions, and a variety of spices. It tastes like slow-cooked campfire stories served with a spoon."

"Careful," Piper warns. "If you describe it like that, the dish might never live up to expectations."

"Has Jenni always been this romantic about food?" Niko asks the girls.

They share a glance and, in unison, say, "Yep, pretty much."

"Heaven forbid a woman enjoys food," I joke.

"Oh, trust me, it's one of my favorite things about you," Niko says.

As we wait for our food, Piper, Sarah, and Niko talk and laugh as if they've known each other forever. My heart could burst into a thousand rays of sunlight.

When the food comes, the green chili is just as scrumptious as I hoped it would be. And the pepper jack bits in the sour-dough rolls add a special kick when dipped in the chili.

"We're coming back here for more tomorrow, right?" Niko asks.

"I don't know. I've got you on a tight schedule, but I'll see what we can do." I wink at him and he smiles back.

Niko sets his gaze on Piper and Sarah across the table. "Tell me about the inn you're opening. I've heard so much from Jenni, but I want to hear it from you."

The girls share a look. Was that trepidation?

"Well, we have an inn," Piper says. "We'll see if we can get it open in a few weeks."

Sarah looks down at her plate, silently. *Crap.* Something has happened. Something she feels responsible for.

"Don't worry, Sarah," I say. "You guys are in amazing shape. You're just overwhelmed because what's left is a dozen small tasks instead of a few big ones."

"I hope you're right," Sarah says. "I think it's starting to hit us that this isn't just some fun renovation project. It is a business we actually have to manage."

Her shoulders tense, and Piper rubs her temples. I can tell they are really feeling the stress right now.

"Well, maybe I can help," Niko offers. "Do you have the basics for opening day? Cleaning staff, a cook, running water? I'm sure you've sorted your PMS?"

I choke on my drink. "Excuse me? What did you ask them?"

"PMS, property management system. It's the software you use to manage room assignments, billing, and check-ins." Niko looks at me, confused.

I turn to Piper and Sarah, who must have known what he was talking about. However, judging by the amusement on their faces, they also caught on to what I found so shocking.

"Sorry," I giggle. "I thought he was asking about your menstrual cycles."

The look of embarrassment on Niko's face makes all three of us laugh until we cry.

Finally, Piper continues the conversation with a healthy dose of the tension wiped away. "Yes, we do. We also have our liquor license, our laundry service, and our snack counter filled up."

"We just don't have blankets," Sarah interrupts, and then shoves her face into her hands.

No wonder they have long faces. This has been plaguing them.

"I've been scouring the internet and local stores, but no one can get us what I want in time. They're all sold out or have the wrong sizes."

"How many do you need?" Niko asks.

"Ten, but a few extra would be amazing in case of emergency."

Niko raises his eyebrows. "That shouldn't be too hard. I can recommend a few suppliers, and we'll get it taken care of in no time."

I squeeze his hand under the table, my heart swelling with pride at the casual way he has referred to my little family as a "we." He's part of us all already, and not an outsider just passing through.

"That's the thing, I don't want basic white hotel linens," Sarah says. "I know it makes the most sense, but I really want something unique. Piper has given me a week to get something secured before we give in and order from a supplier."

Piper shifts in her chair, her eyes looking anywhere but at Sarah.

"That's awesome, Sarah," I say, trying to smooth over the discomfort I'm sensing. "I can't wait to see what you come up with."

By the time we get home to my apartment, Niko is half asleep. We collapse in bed, and I sleep more soundly than I have in months.

15

Niko

BUENA VISTA, COLORADO
EARLY DECEMBER

Jet lag is a drag. But the frosted valleys of Buena Vista are absolutely gorgeous. I've been up since 3 a.m., unable to fall back to sleep, but my eyes are glued to the views. Jenni's car weaves down the highway, alongside a river that has yet to ice over, despite little pockets of snow that haven't melted in the shady spots. We pass red and gold fields of dried grass, dotted with red barns and blue farmhouses. It's different from the roadside views of Greece or Southern California.

"Tell me again where we're headed?" I ask Jenni.

"We're going to visit a client's hot springs resort," she says. "We should be there in ten minutes. It's a natural thermal spring fed from underground water. They have pools and tubs filled from the spring. I've written dozens of ad campaigns for this place, but I've never been."

That sounds cool. And it's just what I need for my sore

back after that flight yesterday. As many times as I have flown back and forth from Europe, I will never get used to how cramped and tight my body feels afterward. Totally worth it, though, to be here with Jenni.

"Do you see that mountain over there?" Jenni asks. "There are some really amazing hikes over there. The rock formations are incredible."

"Cool, maybe we can go next summer," I say, realizing what I was saying as soon as it was out of my mouth. We currently don't have plans to be here next summer, and I don't want to give her any hints about my plan to stay.

"Yeah, it would be great if you came and visited next summer," she says, a thrum of excitement in her voice. "Or maybe I'll have to visit Greece. I know you're busiest during the summer."

"I'm sure we'll figure something out," I say, not wanting to commit to something I know won't happen. I want to keep my plans of moving here a surprise for Christmas morning.

After speaking with Ana, I created a game of envelopes for Jenni to uncover her surprise. I've written riddles on postcards from our favorite memories from the island. Each riddle tells her which envelope to open next. Eventually, she'll get to a postcard of the "Colorful Colorado" state welcome sign that I bought when I got off the plane in Denver. On the back, I've written: "I'm ready to make more memories in Colorado. Will you have me?"

It's incredibly cheesy, but as Ana said, if Jenni's visit to Mykonos taught her anything, hopefully it's that I love a grand gesture.

Jenni turns off the main road and drives a short distance up to the hot springs. When I step out of the car, I'm chilled by the cool mountain air. The hot springs resort is perched on a rocky cliffside, flanked by pine trees on one side and gorgeous views of the valley below on the other.

"Welcome," a woman says as we walk into the reception building.

"Hi, we have a reservation under Swanson," Jenni tells her.

"Of course! One of our couples' tubs. Have you been here before?"

"We haven't," I say. "But I've heard amazing things. You guys must have a killer marketing team."

I wink at Jenni, causing her to blush.

"I'm sure we do," the woman says, a hint of confusion in her voice. "If you'll follow me, I'll show you to the locker rooms. Once you change, head outside and follow the signs to tub thirteen. You'll find everything you need there."

I leave Jenni at the women's locker room door and head into the men's. After changing into my bathing suit, I don a plush robe and slippers. I wait for Jenni outside the locker rooms. From where I'm standing, I see six different pools. There are three communal pools and three smaller tubs meant for private parties. At the far end, a set of stairs leads into the trees and the rest of the tubs, I presume. Steam wafts up the path, making the whole area look like a mystical garden.

I can see my breath as I wait and pull the robe more tightly around myself. It's cold, and I can't wait to dip into the hot water.

"You got ready quick," Jenni says after exiting the women's locker room.

"I couldn't wait," I tell her and pull her in for a kiss. I want to hold onto her forever, to feel her warmth. "Are you ready?"

"I am. Let's go find this tub."

We walk, hand in hand, following the stairs to tub thirteen. Once we reach the tub, we find a barrel with two small cupboard doors holding ear muffs, a towel warmer, a bottle of champagne, and two plastic champagne flutes.

"Should I be worried that you're going to hide these from me if I take my eyes off of them?" I ask, remembering the adorable look on Jenni's face when I caught her red-handed trying to hide the complimentary champagne on our catamaran in Mykonos.

"I don't know. Depends on your behavior," she says with a smirk. "You have to earn champagne."

"Oh yeah? Put me to work, boss."

She laughs, and it's the best sound in the world.

I help Jenni out of her robe and remove my own before placing both of them in the towel warmer. We slip into the scalding tub. I take my time submerging, but Jenni plunges straight in. "Aren't you hot?"

"Isn't that the point?" she asks. "Come on, it feels so good."

She leans back against the rock wall of the tub and moans. She looks beautiful. This whole place is beautiful. From our tub, we have a clear view of natural stone formations and the Rocky Mountains in the distance.

I slide further into the water next to Jenni. The water smells distinctly like Sulphur, but it's not nearly as bad as I expected.

"This is perfect," Jenni says, as if she read my mind. "How do you feel?"

"I feel great," I say, letting my muscles relax.

"You should install a hot spring tub at the Omorfiá," she says, her eyes closed.

I laugh. "I don't think there are any natural springs on the island," I tell her.

"That's a shame. Because this is heaven."

Our view is fantastic. It's quiet and peaceful as the sun shines between the trees. She's right, this is heaven.

I look at Jenni. Her wavy brown hair is pulled up into a bun on top of her head, and she's not wearing any makeup. She seems like she could fall asleep.

I love you.

The words pop into my head out of nowhere. I can't say that to Jenni. We've been together for a few months, but the time we've physically spent together has been so short. What if she's not ready? What if she thinks I'm jumping the gun?

When I think about what she means to me, and all the times I've waited by the phone or agonized over the perfect text to send, I don't think it's too soon. I do love her. I love her more than I've loved anyone.

I can't think about that right now. It would be completely crazy to say something like that right after we reconnect. What if she doesn't say it back?

"So how am I going to earn that champagne?" I ask, instead. "I could tell you that you're the most beautiful woman I've ever seen." I rub her hand in mine under the water. "Or I could give you a massage. What about reciting poetry?"

"All three?" she requests, with a smile spreading between rosy cheeks.

I should have thought this through. I don't know any poetry, unless you count a nursery rhyme.

"Jenni, you are the most beautiful woman I have ever seen," I start. "This place is stunning, but it wouldn't be half as gorgeous without you here."

I pull her in for a kiss, and she wraps her arms around me. It reminds me of our first kiss in Mykonos when we were swimming in the sea. I look back on that day, wondering what came over me. I behaved in a way that was so unprofessional. But my heart was drawn to Jenni in a way I couldn't explain, as if she were my missing piece. She made me feel whole and experience life in three dimensions again. Then she went home, and my life just hasn't been the same since.

"That's a start," Jenni says. "And the massage, please."

I pull her in front of me, and she rests against my chest. I gently knead her shoulders, making sure not to press too hard. A surprising number of knots litter her neck and back. "You feel tense," I tell her. "Have you been stressed about something?"

"What?" She yanks her body away from me, and I regret saying anything. "No, I don't think so. What would I have to be stressed about?"

I don't know what nerve I just hit, but she is not comfortable with that question. At all. Is she hiding something? Why is she so defensive about being stressed?

"Sorry, I didn't mean it in a bad way," I tell her, reaching for her shoulder. "I'm sure it's just from helping the girls with the inn and the holidays. That's all."

"Yeah," she says, almost as if she's trying to convince herself. "You're probably right. That would make sense."

She returns to her spot, and I massage her arms, rather than her shoulders. She melts into me, restoring our perfect moment. I place kisses on her neck as I work my way down her arms. Eventually, I wrap my arms around her, and she rests her head on my shoulder. We sit in silence, enjoying the water.

"I want to stay here forever," I tell her.

"Me too," she says, without opening her eyes.

A warmth grows in my chest, hoping she'll respond the same way when I tell her I'm staying for good.

Jenni twists to face me, a smile beaming on her face. "Is it time for the poetry?"

"Okay, give me a second to think," I tell her.

I look into her eyes, and I am completely lost for words, but not in a romantic way. Call it stage fright or writer's block, but not a single rhyme comes to mind.

Finally, I go with the oldest rhyme in the book. "Roses are red, violets are blue," I say, and pause, desperate to come up with a second stanza. "This day has been perfect, and so have you."

She radiates sunshine, her mood shifting from the awkward exchange a minute ago. "That, my friend, has earned you some champagne."

I pump my fist in celebration before climbing out of the

steaming water. I retrieve the bottle and glasses, then pop the cork and pour.

When I return to the tub and hand Jenni her glass, she raises it in a toast.

"To another magical trip," she declares. "May our weeks in Colorado be filled with as much adventure as the ones we spent in Greece."

I clink my glass with hers, the plastic making a dull sound.

And to many more weeks like it, I silently add.

16

Sarah

Twinkling lights are strung along Main Street. Snow machines pump flurries into the air, and baristas from Bobby's Café are passing out hot chocolate and coffee to everyone, filling the air with the scent of peppermint and cocoa. The four of us have found a spot in the middle of the route to watch the annual Pineview Springs Holiday Parade.

"Here, take a blanket," Jenni says, handing over a large wool blanket for Piper and me before wrapping another one around herself and Niko.

"Oh, this is amazing, thank you," Piper tells her and moves next to me, draping the thick blanket around our shoulders.

Bobby stops by and hands each of us a hot chocolate. He's dressed in a festive apron with Christmas cookies printed all over it and a Santa hat. "Make sure you girls stay for the whole parade, okay, there's a surprise coming," he says, with a wink at Jenni. "But I've got to run, the parade's about to start."

"That was weird," I tell the group. "Do you know what Bobby was talking about?"

Piper shrugs her shoulders under our blanket. "No clue."

We both turn to look at Jenni. She makes a face that says, "Me neither."

I have the strange feeling she's hiding something, but I have no idea what it could be. We settle in and sip our cocoa, watching as the crowd splits and settles in on either side of the street.

The parade starts with the high school marching band. They are dressed in their full uniforms, with red and white tinsel wrapped around their tall hats. The band is small, but "Deck the Halls" rings out through the cold air.

"Do you think their lips are going to freeze to their instruments?" Niko asks, leaning over to ask us.

"I think it's possible," Piper says. "Can you imagine getting your lips stuck to a trombone?"

"You guys are so weird," Jenni chimes in, laughing.

As the band marches on, I take a sip of my hot chocolate and watch as Niko sneaks glances at Jenni, kissing her forehead and hanging on her every word. Jenni was so worried the other day when we were making decorations for the inn, but I don't see signs of anything but love between them. It's nauseating.

I'm a little jealous. I hate myself for feeling it, but I do. I know Jenni is feeling insecure right now, but the way Niko is treating her and the fact that they can spend this time together devoid of responsibility is enviable. Piper and I haven't had a conversation free of worry about the inn in months. Even when we are laughing over misplaced tiles in the bathroom, there is always an underlying tension about whether we will complete everything on time and what else is on the to-do list.

And then, of course, there is the RV. After our conversation the other day, she seems determined to keep it. I did not expect her to be the one resisting selling it over sentimental reasons. I feel the same way, of course, but I also know that it's the only way I'm going to afford that ring.

When did our lives become so complicated? I miss the days when all we worried about was making sure we had a stable internet connection at the next campground. Was all of this a mistake? Will our relationship survive in this more complex life?

I lean into Piper, needing her physical comfort to reassure me that we're okay. She puts an arm around my shoulder under the blanket and rubs my arm as we watch the next group of children march in the parade. They are from a local scouting group and are dressed in mismatched reindeer horns and red noses. A few are ringing sleigh bells and shouting "Merry Christmas." Their faces beam in the light of the parade as they throw candy canes to the crowd.

"Did you ever participate in the parade?" I ask Piper. I don't remember her ever talking about it.

"No, I wasn't involved in anything normal enough to join the parade," she laughs. "I think Jenni walked a few times. Right?" She leans past me to Jenni and Niko, who are whispering to each other and not paying any attention to us.

"What?" Jenni asks when Piper calls her name.

"Were you ever in the parade as a kid?" I ask, smiling because she looks so happy.

"Once or twice with my agriculture group. It was a total blast."

A candy cane comes flying at us, and Niko puts a hand in front of Jenni's face, catching it. He hands it to a little kid to his right.

We turn back to the parade as a few pickup trucks drive by with sparkling lights and blaring Christmas music. A man in a Santa suit sits in the bed of the last truck, tossing out goody bags to the children lining the curb on either side of Main Street. It's cute to see the magic in their eyes as they hope to get a bag of treats.

After a few more groups go by, the grand marshal float pulls up. The entire parade route is only about five blocks, and we're right in the middle. The float stops right in front of us. The mayor will conduct a short ceremony and officially light up the town's Christmas lights. The grand marshal will be thanked for his contributions this year, and next year's grand marshal will be announced.

The mayor stands and thanks everyone for coming out to the parade. "Our town is special, and I think you all know that. This year's light display is sponsored by none other than our Grand Marshal Bobby from Bobby's Café."

The mayor hands the microphone over to Bobby, who is still dressed in his festive baker's outfit.

"Thank you, Mayor," Bobby says. "We'll light the street in a moment, but first, I want to make sure that you all know you can stop in any time at Bobby's Café for festive holiday treats. We have eggnog lattes, peppermint coffee, frosted candy cane frappes, and the biggest gingerbread cookies around."

The crowd cheers, and Bobby continues, "And I hope to see you at the rest of the town's festivities. The café will have a booth at the opening of the ice-skating rink at the lake. I am also thrilled to announce that we'll be providing hot beverages at the grand reopening of the Pineview Inn on December 22nd. It's going to be an amazing event."

Applause echoes on the street, once more. I sneak a glance at Piper. She looks like she's going to be ill. She hates the attention. I look to see what she's staring at, and it's not the float or Bobby. She's watching an angry man across the street. He's throwing his hands up and saying something to a few other men. Their wives are all huddled together ignoring the scene their husbands are making.

I nudge Jenni with my elbow and whisper, "Who is that over there?"

"Ugh, that's Charlie. We had a run-in with him the other night before dinner. He's always angry about something."

I've never heard of Charlie, but his presence is affecting Piper. "What's his deal?" I ask Jenni.

"Who knows. He doesn't like change."

Then why does Piper look so pale in the face? Jenni hasn't noticed how upset Piper looks. I don't want to draw attention to it, so instead I nudge my girlfriend. "Are you okay?"

"Yeah," she responds without taking her eyes off the other side of the street.

From the float, Bobby calls for a drumroll for the lights. The crowd all starts drumming on their thighs, and with a wave of Bobby's hands, multicolored lights illuminate the buildings lining the street. Lights in the shape of bows, snowmen, and sleigh bells cover the brick walls.

Everyone's faces light up, reflecting the dazzling display.

I slip my hand into Piper's gloved hand. "Are you sure you're okay? Did that guy say something to you recently?"

"Who?" She cocks an eyebrow. I guess she didn't realize how noticeable her behavior had been.

"Charlie, that guy you're staring at across the street. Jenni says he's a jerk."

She meets my eyes for the first time. "No," she refutes. "No, Charlie hasn't said anything to me. I haven't talked to him in years."

I get the feeling she's lying, but I drop the subject. If she wanted me to know, I guess she would tell me. I just hope she isn't bottling things up and trying to take everything on by herself.

After the mayor says a few more words, the music resumes, and the float starts to move down the street with Bobby and the new grand marshal, whom I don't recognize, waving at the crowd.

"Wouldn't it be cool if we were chosen as the grand marshals someday? They can have two, right? That would be so fun to help with the parade."

Piper guffaws. "Yeah, I'm not going to hold my breath, but maybe someday."

I deflate. I guess she's not feeling much better about the community and our place in it.

When the parade is over, Niko and Jenni suggest we all go for drinks. I look at Piper to see what she thinks.

"I don't think so," she says. "We have a lot of work to do tomorrow at the inn. Why don't we head home and get some rest?"

"You guys have fun," I tell them. "Don't do anything we wouldn't do."

"Impossible," Jenni says. "You're the rowdiest bunch I know." She laughs.

We hug our goodbyes and go our separate ways.

The car ride back to the inn is silent, and when we go to bed, Piper pulls out her computer and says she's going to work for a bit. I don't know what spooked her earlier, but she isn't willing to talk about it.

I give her a kiss goodnight and roll over to read my book.

17

Piper

PINEVIEW SPRINGS, COLORADO
MID DECEMBER

"Good news!" Sarah shouts as she comes up the front walkway of the inn.

I startle, but thankfully don't fall from the ladder I'm using to string Christmas lights on the eaves. We went back and forth on color and style for weeks, but eventually landed on white icicle lights. They're a bit 2010, but they were cheap and will complement nicely if we ever get any snow.

"Oh yeah? What's that?" I call down, one hand on the roof and the other holding the lights. I'd rather not climb down if I don't have to.

"I found comforters!" Sarah shouts, looking so proud of herself.

I loop the light strand over the top rung of the ladder and climb down as quickly as possible. "No way! Where?"

"Online. I found a company in Utah that makes custom,

reversible linen duvet covers in natural colors. I called them, and a woman helped me pick complementary colors so we can mix and match the blankets with the sheets and pillows. She promised they would be done in a week, and then they'd ship them with next-day delivery."

"Did you also order the duvets? Or just the covers?" My brain is refusing to get excited about this until I have all of the information.

"I did!" Sarah says, grinning from ear to ear. "We did it. We will have beds *and* gorgeous bedding for our guests in time to open."

"We will have beds *and* gorgeous bedding for our guests in time to open," I repeat, barely believing the words coming out of my mouth.

We scream and suddenly we're holding hands and jumping in circles around the front of the property.

I wrap Sarah in my arms. "I'm sorry," I tell her.

"Sorry for what?" Her eyebrows knit together as she locks eyes with me.

"That I haven't been more supportive of you throughout this process. You have done so much to make this place a home, not just a business. You deserve all your dreams to come true. Even when I think it's easier to order plain white comforters."

Sarah takes a step back, biting her lips. "No. Don't apologize. If I had listened to you, this would have been taken care of weeks or months ago, and we wouldn't need to be dancing around the front lawn because we finally found some. I should be more realistic, like you."

My gut twists. I hate that I make her feel that way. "I—"

"Hello," a shrill voice calls from the small parking lot adjacent to the inn. Sarah and I turn toward the voice. It's familiar, but I can't quite place it.

When my eyes land on them, I cringe. Two of the biggest busybodies in town. What do they want?

"Patty, Kathy, hi!" I say. "What can we do for you?"

Patty and Kathy aren't sisters, but you would never know that by looking at them. They share the same gray-brown shag hairstyle and are always wearing crewneck sweatshirts from the national parks.

"Oh, nothing," Kathy says, nonchalantly, as if they were just driving by and wanted to stop for a chat. "We just thought we would stop by and see how you girls are getting on with the inn. Your big opening is soon, right? Is everything ready?"

Her sweet voice is anything but accusatory. Still, my defenses go into overdrive. I know what these women are like and how they talk. If we show any sign of weakness, pretty soon the word around town will be that we've failed before we even open the doors.

"We're doing great and can't wait to welcome everyone. Will you be joining us for the grand opening? You won't want to miss it. We're going to have food, drinks, and a tree lighting celebration."

"Of course, we wouldn't miss it," Patty chimes in. "We're so excited for the reopening. Any chance for a sneak peek at the inside? I'm dying to see what you've done."

Panic sets in. A sneak peek? We can't. But how can we turn away Patty and Kathy? They are Pineview Springs royalty, and maybe the only people who could refute Charlie LeGrande. If they were to go back to their friends and rave about the inn, it could put all of his grumbling to rest. Then again, if they said it was a mess, it could ruin us. But that's a risk I'm willing to take.

"You know, it's not quite ready—" Sarah starts to say.

"We can show them a few rooms," I say, and give Sarah an apologetic look for cutting her off. "Anything for you! How about I take you inside?"

"That would be lovely," Patty says, grabbing her glasses from where they dangle on her chest, attached to a beaded necklace.

"We've just been so anxious to see all the improvements!" Kathy calls out. The way she says "improvements" makes me wonder whether she believes the changes are for the better or not. My chest constricts with nerves.

We walk through the lobby, which smells like fresh paint. The hardwood floor is mopped, and the rug is pristine. "You'll find we haven't changed much," I say. "We want the feel of the inn to be cozy and reminiscent of old mountain lodges, just like when the Harpers were here. We even saved their old wooden rocking chairs. They are in the shed right now until all the other furniture is moved in."

The two women take a walk around the room, which feels spacious without the furniture or guests milling about. The women nod appraisingly.

"Through here, we have a small lodge area that overlooks the woods." It's a room with floor-to-ceiling glass windows, a wood-burning fireplace, and leather chairs around an old wooden table.

"Oh, imagine sitting here watching a deer walk by through the trees," Kathy coos.

"What about the guest rooms?" Patty asks. "Can we see one?"

Damn. I was hoping to take them to the kitchen or out on the patio. But if they want to look at a guest room, I have no choice but to oblige. The town's acceptance of the inn is at stake.

"Of course," I tell them. "They aren't completely made up yet, but we can look at a room."

Sarah stares at me with wide eyes. From behind the women's backs, she mouths, "What are you doing?"

I smile and do my best to reassure her that I haven't lost my mind. They can't expect the beds to be made up and tissue boxes to be in place when we don't open for two more weeks. The housekeeping team hasn't even started working yet. Regardless, my hands are shaking as I open the door to the first guest room on the second floor.

The room features a queen-sized bed with an ornate wooden frame, a small dresser with painted drawers, and a large window overlooking the trees. Hopefully, by the time we open, the trees will be dusted with snow, but for now, the evergreens glisten in the sunshine.

"Oh, it's a bit dusty in here, isn't it?" Patty asks, running a finger on the dresser. "Do you need any help with that?"

I can't help but feel the judgment lacing her words like acid in my stomach. Of course, she noticed. "No, no help needed. We have a great housekeeping staff starting a few days before we open. They'll get everything cleaned up and make it guest-ready." If we cleaned it now, we would just have to clean again before the big day.

"That makes sense. We know these old cabins are always dusty, no matter what you do," Kathy says. "That must be why you don't have the bedding on yet."

Sarah, whom I didn't realize had followed us into the room, clears her throat. "That's a funny story, actually! We have had the hardest time finding comforters, but—"

"But we have them!" I finish for her. I will not let these women spread the news that we don't even have bedding yet. "They are being cleaned to get the factory smell out, but they are beautiful. You will have to book a stay. We are offering a staycation discount for locals who make a reservation within the first year. Let's go downstairs and get you a flyer."

"Oh, I love a discount," Patty says. "But wait, what was the funny story?"

I usher the two women out of the room and send an apologetic look over my shoulder to Sarah. Hopefully, she understands why I had to cut her off. "Oh, it's hilarious. The company accidentally sent us the wrong size, and we ended up with ten twin-sized duvet covers. Luckily, we got it all taken care of."

I hope I don't sound as skittish as I feel. I won't give these women any ammunition to think poorly of the inn or Sarah. She won't suffer the way I did when I was a kid. I have to protect her.

"Oh my, that would be a problem," Patty says with a chuckle. "But you have all the right sizes now?"

"Yep, all ten, queen-sized quilts. Plus a few extra, just in case."

She looks at me with her eyes narrowed. "Perfect."

I end this impromptu tour as we head down the stairs. "Let me walk you out to the car. Unfortunately, Sarah and I need to get back to hanging these lights and steaming the wrinkles out of the drapes."

"That reminds me!" Kathy says with a note of urgency. "The whole reason we came over is that we wanted to bring you a few boxes of Christmas decorations. All the ladies went through their basements and found a few things to donate. We know how expensive everything is these days."

The women rush to their car and unload boxes filled with wreaths, snowman table decorations, faux garland, and vintage Christmas ornaments.

I pick up a round, glass ornament with hand-painted blue spruce trees covered in snow. "This is all so lovely. We couldn't possibly take it." My voice catches in my throat as I set the ornament back into the box.

"Yes, you can," Patty says. "It's yours. We don't need it, and it would make everyone so happy to see these decorations at the inn instead of boxed up in our basements."

Her words lick at wounds that have festered in my heart for

a long time. A small ember of hope flickers to life, despite my suspicions about their motives.

"Thank you," I finally say. "I really appreciate it."

"Don't say another word. Is there anything else we can help you with?" Kathy asks.

Even though Patty and Kathy are showing support now, it doesn't mean they won't turn on us at the first sign of trouble, and I need them singing our praises.

"Cleaning? Flyers? More decorations?" Patty asks, while I'm still thinking. "I'm sure we could scrounge through our donation boxes and find all sorts of things."

We don't need decorations. Sarah has been collecting decor pieces for each room nonstop since we bought the inn. I can't think of anything else we would need.

Books.

Everyone has books they want to get rid of, don't they? We could use them for the RV bookshop. Everyone loves a used bookstore—cheaper prices, sustainability, the romance of turning pages that have touched other hearts.

"Actually, there might be one thing," I say, glancing back at the inn to make sure Sarah hasn't followed us out. "I'm trying to surprise Sarah with a little used bookshop at the inn. Would you have some books you could donate?"

Both women cover their hearts and sigh in unison. "That's so sweet," Patty says.

"Say no more," Kathy tells me. "We will spread the word far and wide that the inn needs books."

I panic. Far and wide is not what I need. "Please make sure no one tells Sarah," I plead. "I really want it to be a surprise."

Kathy mimes locking her lips and tossing the key over her shoulder. Patty nods and says, "Your secret is safe with us."

And that's when I realize how much I've risked. The knitting ladies are notorious gossips. If Sarah doesn't find out about the bookshop from someone, it will be a Christmas miracle.

18

Niko

BRECKENRIDGE, COLORADO
MID DECEMBER

One benefit of my ongoing jet lag is that, even though I've been in Colorado for a week now, I still woke up early enough this morning to sneak away and pick up coffee and donuts before Jenni wakes up. I've been visiting Bobby's Café nearly every morning.

When I get back, we eat breakfast in bed and sip our drinks until I show her exactly how much I have missed her. Mid-morning, we make our way to Breckenridge in a cozy haze of holiday cheer.

Mornings like this confirm that I am making the right decision to leave the hotel. I don't want to be apart from Jenni again.

"Earth to Niko," Jenni says from the driver's seat of her Subaru. "We're here."

Jenni's voice shakes me from a daydream of picturing our

life together here. A large part of me wants to blurt out that I am moving here to be with her, for good. The secret is burning a hole in my pocket.

"Sorry," I respond. "I must still be a little jet-lagged." Jenni hasn't mentioned any of our plans for today, so I don't even know where here is.

"Do you want to go home? We don't have to do any of this," Jenni says, grabbing my hand on the center console.

"Are you kidding me? I wouldn't want to be anywhere else."

Jenni rolls her eyes with a smile. She clearly doesn't realize how much I mean it. It isn't a platitude. It's a certainty.

We climb out of the car, and I realize we are at an ice rink. "Wait, I thought we weren't skating for a few more days?"

"We're not. We're just using the parking lot," she tells me. "We're here to see a troll."

"A troll?"

"Yep! You took me to see a dragon, which I still don't think looks like a dragon, so I'm taking you to see a troll."

"I can't wait," I say. "And the island does look like a dragon. We were looking from the wrong angle."

"Keep telling yourself that." Jenni pats me on the chest as she takes my hand and pulls me toward the far corner of the parking lot. I stand steady, pulling her into me instead. I wrap my arms around her and kiss her. I have to take every chance I can get. Her gloved hands come to the back of my neck, warming it from the winter air.

A moment later, she's pulling free. "Niko, are you okay? You're shaking. You aren't afraid of trolls, are you?"

I crack a smile. I was hoping she wouldn't notice that I am freezing. This is not the Mediterranean winter that I'm used to. "Not afraid of trolls, just turning into a snowman, but it's all good."

"Here," she says, unwrapping a pink and orange scarf from around her neck and wrapping it around mine.

"I thought you would never offer," I say, adjusting the scarf. "It's just my color."

She laughs and places a kiss on my cheek. "Good. Now let's go. Walking will warm you up."

We come upon a trailhead in the corner of the parking lot. The trail sign is painted with arrows pointing into the trees and reads "Troll This Way."

"Are we going to cross some sort of fairy tale bridge by outsmarting a troll?" I ask.

"Nope! You'll see."

It's great to see Jenni in this environment. She's so confident and comfortable. The complete opposite of the woman in Greece, who was scared of expressing any opinion. I absolutely love seeing her this way. "Okay. Lead the way."

We walk along the trail holding hands until we see a line of people ahead.

"We must be getting close. Everyone wants to stop and take pictures once they get there," Jenni says.

"Are you going to tell me what this troll thing is about, now?" I ask. I'm standing on my tiptoes trying to see what everyone is taking pictures of, but there are too many trees blocking my view.

"Nope, it's better if you're surprised. But *you* can tell me about springtime in Mykonos. When does it start getting warmer? I've been thinking about my next visit. When should I come?"

Jenni leans her head against my chest, and I put my hand on her shoulder. "Oh, it will still be winter in Mykonos for a while, but tourism should start to pick up in April or so."

"So if I come visit before then, I'll have you mostly to myself?" Jenni smiles.

I hesitate. I can't answer that question without giving away my plans. I won't be in Greece anytime between now and April if things go as planned. I don't want to lie to her if I can help it. I shouldn't let her plan a trip she won't ever go on.

We take a few steps as the line moves forward. "You can have me all to yourself any time you want. Just say the word." I wink at her.

"Could we travel a bit? Maybe go to Athens, where your family is, and see the rest of the country?"

"Someday. But are you sure you want to visit that soon?" I ask. "It's such a long way to travel, and you have so many things going on here."

"Of course, I do! I want to see you, and there are so many things I still have lots to do in Greece."

She is not making this easy.

"True," I tell her, as we take a few more steps. "But there's so much here, too. Maybe I can come back to Colorado before the resort gets really busy."

Jenni looks at me, confusion clouding her gaze. She can tell I'm being noncommittal and looks like she's about to ask why. I try to diffuse the situation in the only way I know how. I lean down and kiss her. "I don't want you to feel any pressure. We can talk about it, but right now, we're here to see a troll."

She turns away from me, toward the line of people. We are getting close, and I can see that a giant wooden statue of a troll has been built into the hillside. The troll towers over the trail, with a potbelly and giant legs extending out toward the crowd of people waiting to take pictures.

"I've never seen anything like this. It's hilarious." I smile at Jenni. "Where did it come from?"

The body is covered in multicolored wooden shingles, and the face features elaborately carved eyes and a nose. One arm is wrapped around a tree, as if he's holding a hiking stick.

Jenni takes a few more steps, barely looking at me. "A

sculptor from Denmark, I think. His name is Thomas Dambo."

I need to lighten the mood. "The troll? That's a pretty anti-climactic name for a troll. He needs a strong name from the Middle Ages."

"No," Jenni says, a smile breaking through her icy expression. "The sculptor's name is Thomas. The troll is named Isak Heartstone."

Relief pours through me as she laughs. "See? That's a good troll name! Looks like we're up next."

Jenni hands her phone to the next person in line and asks them to take our photo in front of the troll. We walk up to take our place between his outstretched legs and smile for the camera.

"Wait, can you take one more?" I ask.

The person with Jenni's phone nods, so I throw Jenni over my shoulder, pretending like we're running away from the statue. After they've taken the photo, I set Jenni down amongst her fit of giggles. "Sorry, I had to. When I see a giant troll, I have to protect what I love."

She stops laughing and looks at me wide-eyed. I hold her gaze, hoping she'll say it back. But before either of us can say anything else, the person behind us in line clears their throat and extends their hand.

"Sorry!" Jenni apologizes, then rushes away from me and grabs her phone. "Come on, let's go. We need to hurry if we want to get lunch before my next surprise."

Epic failure.

I tried to tell Jenni I loved her, and she looked at me as if I were speaking a foreign language. Why can't I do anything right on this trip?

Jenni leads me out of the ice rink parking lot and toward Main Street. I scold myself as we walk. I've gotten ahead of myself. I knew I was moving too quickly. I should have listened to my instincts at the hot springs. If I scare her off, it could jeopardize everything.

After a few minutes of small talk, Jenni leads me into a small courtyard and down a set of stairs into a dark basement. "What is this place?"

As my eyes adjust, Jenni grabs my hand. "This is one of my favorite spots in Breck. It's an American diner joint with a full arcade."

As my eyes adjust, I see rows of arcade machines to the right and a restaurant to the left. I haven't played arcade video games in ages. Maybe I can challenge Jenni to a round of Pac-Man after we eat.

Once we're at our table, I grab a menu.

"I know how much you miss American pizza. That's why I chose this place. They make a great pizza. We can have any toppings you want," she says.

My stomach growls. I hadn't been feeling hungry, but at the thought of pizza, I'm suddenly ravenous. I run my eyes down the list. "This one sounds good," I say, and point to a specialty pizza loaded with peppers, mushrooms, sausage, and pepperoni.

"Good choice," Jenni says and flags down a waiter. Before he can reach the table, though, Jenni's phone rings.

"I should probably answer this. Can you order?" she asks as she answers. "Hi, Mom. How are you? How's Seattle?"

I hope nothing is wrong. Jenni nods and turns toward the wall while I place our order with the waiter. When he walks away, she turns back and puts the phone on speaker.

"I just got a phone call from Kathy, and she said she was worried about Piper and Sarah," Jenni's mom says.

"Worried how? Did something happen?" Jenni asks.

"I guess they went over to check out the inn, and the girls got really cagey and nervous when they mentioned bedding."

Jenni lets out an exasperated sigh. "Mom, can your friends ever mind their own business?"

"They weren't trying to be nosy. They are concerned," her mom says. "They wanted me to confirm if the girls have bedding for the inn? Aren't they opening soon?"

"They have had a few issues with the bedding, but it's fine; they can handle it. They have sheets and pillows, and their comforters should be here any day now."

I watch as Jenni navigates this conversation like a pro. She knows her mom worries about everything, but she has to protect her friends.

An audible gasp escapes the phone. "They don't have them yet? Jenni, this isn't Denver. It's the mountains. Nothing is delivered when it is supposed to be, especially this time of year. What if a storm comes? Or the truck is delayed?"

I know Jenni is sticking up for her friends, but I'm Team Mom on this one. If I were in Piper and Jenni's shoes right now, I'd be pretty worried and would order the easiest option.

"Mom, stop. I won't micromanage them. They are grownups and they will figure this out on their own."

"But honey, what if—"

"Hi, Mrs. Swanson, Niko here," I interrupt. I want to put an end to this before Jenni gets so annoyed that it ruins the rest of the afternoon. I don't want any more hiccups today. "I know it sounds intimidating, but things can work quickly in the hospitality industry. Suppliers in Denver can deliver hotel linens directly from the warehouse in a matter of days."

"Oh, hi, Niko!" she says, changing her tone. "I didn't realize you were there. How was your flight?"

Jenni flashes me a grateful smile. "Mom, we're actually on a date right now. We'll call you tonight. Don't worry about the bedding at the inn. Everything will work out."

The look on Jenni's face tattles that she doesn't quite believe her own words.

"Okay, honey, I'm sorry. I'll call Patty back and let them know. Are we still planning to have dinner at our house when we get back?"

"Yes," Jenni says. And I add, "I'm really looking forward to it, Mrs. Swanson."

"Oh, call me Rebecca," Mom says. "Have fun, you two."

Jenni hangs up the phone and returns it to her coat pocket. She shrugs her shoulders, looking at me apologetically.

"Why do I have the feeling she isn't going to tell Patty to stop worrying?" I ask.

Jenni rolls her eyes. "Because worrying is in her DNA," she says.

Just then, the waiter sets our pizza down on a stand in the middle of the table and hands us two plates. It smells incredible, and the crust looks like it's been braided, puffed up, and glazed. Jenni catches me inspecting it.

"Have you ever heard of Colorado-style pizza?" Jenni asks. "The crust is extra thick and brushed with honey before baking."

"Say no more," I say and grab a slice. Before I can put it on a plate to offer Jenni, she pulls a slice straight from the pan to her mouth and takes a hot, steamy bite. Cheese stretches from her lips to the slice in her hands. Grateful that I clearly don't have to be polite with my food, I do the same.

Maybe it's because I haven't had any in a while, but to say this is the best pizza I've ever had would be an understatement. This pizza alone might be enough to make me want to move here. Unless Jenni doesn't reciprocate my feelings. I wouldn't be able to stay in Colorado if she didn't want me here.

19

Jenni

I protect what I love.

Niko's words, and the way he said them with such a meaningful gaze, have been replaying in my head since we took
pictures at the troll. Was he trying to say he loves me? If so,
why did he say it after basically telling me he didn't want me to
visit?

I'm so confused. I barely have an appetite, but I struggle
through the pizza for Niko's sake.

After we eat through about half of the pan, I excuse myself
to the restroom. I need to ask Piper and Sarah what they think.
It's so cliché, and I hate that I'm this desperate for validation,
but considering I have been planning to put my life on hold to
spend the next month in Greece, I need to figure out what's
going on.

I pull up our group chat.

> Jenni: Emergency. I need opinions. I asked Niko about visiting him in Greece, and he brushed me off. He basically told me not to visit him. And it freaked me out.

I wait for the bubbles with three dots to appear. *Please don't be busy*, I silently beg. Then, my phone pings.

> Piper: Are you sure that's what he meant? That doesn't sound like Niko.

> Jenni: He said he didn't want me to feel pressure to visit because my life is here. He was very clear about our lives being in separate places, almost like he doesn't want them to overlap.

> Sarah: That doesn't make sense. Why would he come here if he didn't want a life with you?

Tears prick at my eyes, and I dab them with a paper towel.

> Jenni: That's the weird thing. A few minutes later, he insinuated that he loved me. But he didn't actually say the words.

> Sarah: What? That's huge!

> Jenni: But he didn't SAY it.

> Piper: You should ask him what he meant, then.

> Jenni: I can't ask him. What if he says it isn't a big deal?

> Sarah: Don't listen to Piper. This isn't a business transaction. You have to find a way for him to repeat what he said. Tell him how great it is to have him here and see what he responds with.

Jenni: After what he said about me visiting him? I feel like he'll just be wishy-washy again.

A toilet flushes and I step into a stall, so I'm not in the way of the sink. Sarah and Piper are probably right. I need to have an honest conversation with him. I can't keep going with so much ambiguity.

Jenni: I've got to get back to the table. But you're right, I just need to talk to him. I wish this weren't so hard.

I wash my hands and exit the bathroom. When I return to the table, Niko has paid for our meal and boxed up the last two slices of pizza. "In case we get hungry in the car," he says.

"You mean in case *you* get hungry in the car?" I tease. Niko ate more than half the pizza himself.

"I plead the fifth," he responds. "Do we have time for a quick game before the next activity?"

I glance at the time on my phone. "One or two. I'm warning you right now, I'm terrible at video games."

Five minutes later, I've successfully hustled Niko in Street Fighter, Donkey Kong, and Pac-Man. He looks impressed.

"You seem to have forgotten that my baby brother is a video game designer. Who do you think played with him to help develop those skills?"

"You surprise me all the time," he says, pulling me in for a hug.

It feels like the right moment to ask Niko what he meant earlier, or why he doesn't want me to visit. But I chicken out. I can't face the possibility that he doesn't feel the same way as I do. So instead, we head up the stairs to the light of day and continue with our afternoon. Our next activity is too romantic for me to ruin it with a talk to determine our relationship status.

WHEN WE PULL into the stables a while later, Niko gives me a look. "Are we going for a trail ride? Because I am not wearing the right shoes, and I might freeze to death."

I contemplate pulling his leg and letting him squirm, but that's more Niko's thing than mine. "No, in the winter, they do sleigh rides. We'll have blankets, gloves, and hot chocolate, I think. In the pictures online, everyone has hot chocolate."

He laughs. "I want my money back if there isn't any."

"You didn't even pay for it," I tease.

"I would if you let me," he says, getting out of the car.

He rushes around to open my door, and we walk, hand in hand, to check in for our sleigh ride. They lead us through a hallway and out behind the office to a team of stunning horses yoked to a dark red, painted sleigh. There are four benches in the sleigh, each piled with blankets and hand warmers.

"I think I see the hot chocolate," Niko says, pointing toward a table with insulated paper cups and large drink dispensers. We grab our cocoa and settle in on the last bench, perfectly sized for two.

Niko and I layer blankets and snuggle together for warmth. I can't shake an uneasy feeling about the conversation I need to have with him. I thought it would be best to enjoy our time together and avoid this discussion until the end of his trip, but the more time we spend, the more I realize how deeply my heart is invested.

My heart will break if he doesn't want the same things that I do.

Once everyone takes their seats, we're on the move. The two black horses move majestically down a dirt road, patchily covered in snow.

The sleigh driver holds reins adorned with bells that jingle as we move. "We appreciate your patience with the snow. We haven't had any big storms yet, but hopefully we'll have some soon. Don't worry, as we get off the road and into the woods, you'll get the snowy sleigh ride you were promised."

"Everyone keeps saying that about the storms," Niko says. "Is it unusual for this time of year?"

"Actually, no," I respond. "We rarely have a white Christmas. But we usually have a few snowfalls by now that cover these dirt roads, even if it all melts in town."

"Maybe we'll get lucky this year," he says with a wink. It's just like Niko, the eternal optimist, to think we might get a white Christmas. It would be magical, but I'm not holding my breath.

As we round a bend in the road, the sleigh driver begins his tour. "Breckenridge started as a mining town. Miners settled here during the Pikes Peak Gold Rush in search of riches."

I lean over to Niko and whisper in his ear. "If you ever visit in the summer, we'll go to one of the mines and pan for gold."

"I would love that," he says. The same noncommittal tone he had earlier gnaws at me. Does he really not want to continue visiting each other? If so, what are we even doing here?

Everything has been perfect since he got here, so I had mostly stopped worrying. But now I can't get a straight answer from him about whether we'll see each other again after he goes back to Mykonos.

My heart sinks. I sip my hot chocolate, not wanting to confront the truth.

Our sleigh pulls into a snowy meadow and stops in front of a bench. The snow around it is trodden down with boot prints. "Okay, folks. Welcome to the meadow," our guide says. "We're going to stop here and give the horses a treat for making it up that hill. You can each take a turn feeding them some grain or carrots and get your photo taken if you'd like."

Everyone starts filing out of the sleigh, eager for their turn to get up close to the animals. Niko and I linger at the end of the line under the trees, waiting for our turn.

I can feel a knot in my throat, burning and threatening to simmer over into tears. Why is everything going so wrong? I have to say something. I'm not going to be able to fake that everything is okay. "Niko, about earlier——"

"Don't," he says, putting a finger to my lips. "It's okay. I understand if you don't feel the same way."

Feel the same way about what?

"What do you mean?"

"Jenni, it's fine. I don't want to pressure you. Honestly, I shouldn't have even said it."

Pressure me? I'm the one who has been trying to plan a visit. What would he be pressuring me about? I'm ready to confront him about my visit when I remember. He *was* saying that he loves me. What does that matter if we have no plans to continue visiting?

I want to ask him, but it's our turn to climb onto the bench, so we're face-to-face with the tall horses. The bench wobbles beneath us, and my heart skips a beat. I am so going to fall off this bench. Niko seems perfectly comfortable, of course, but I'm the clumsy one.

I haven't been self-conscious about that in a long time, but the feeling is resurfacing and telling me I'm not good enough. And I hate it.

We stand and smile for the camera. Steam wafts from the horses' nostrils, warming my face, and I can't help but let a tiny tear escape down my cheek. When I planned this outing, I imagined how romantic and sentimental it would be. Now, I'm here on a wobbly bench, with frozen toes and a confused heart.

I reach for a handful of grain from the black bucket hanging from a nearby pole. Something hot and wet swipes up and down my cheek. *What the heck?*

I turn, trying to figure out what Niko is doing. It's a tongue. A hot, sticky, slimy tongue the size of my hand.

The horse just licked me. I'm frozen in shock. Then he does it again, pushing me off balance. I fall off the bench and land right on my butt in the snow, soaking through my pants almost instantly. Niko rushes to help me up, but I brush him off. I'm so tired of needing to be rescued.

Hysterical, painful laughter erupts from my chest. Of course, this would happen to me. I always seem to fall into Niko's arms, and he has to help me up. No wonder he might be growing sick of it.

"Are you okay?"

"Yep," I say, not making eye contact. "Totally fine."

"Do you still want to feed the horses?"

"Yep," I say, again. I grab a carrot and offer my hand to the horse, keeping my cheeks at a safe distance this time. Niko seems hesitant, but grabs a handful of grain and feeds the other horse.

They are beautiful, strong, and stalwart. I wish I could say the same about myself. But it's clear that I'm falling into old patterns.

I don't want to be the girl who beats herself up over someone else's opinions. I have to talk to Niko and figure things out. No matter what his answer might be. I don't do that anymore. It's time to have the difficult conversation and figure out where I stand.

I take a deep breath and steady myself.

"Niko, what did you mean when you said you protect the things you love?"

"Well," he responds, looking sheepish. "I meant that I love you."

My eyes search his face, looking for clues to put these puzzle pieces together. Before I can speak, the bells on the reins jingle. "Climb on up, folks. We have one more cinematic viewing spot to get to before we head back."

Niko takes my hand and helps me step up into the carriage, where we settle once again under the blankets.

"Niko, I … I don't understand."

"What don't you understand? I love you. I have missed you more than anything over the past few months, and being here with you has brought me back to life. It's okay if you aren't ready to say it back. I'm fine waiting."

Then why won't you talk about our future?

The sincerity in his eyes pushes my insecurity aside, at least for now. A subtle warmth, like the sun on an early spring day, fills my chest.

"I love you, too."

Niko takes my face in his hand and kisses me deeply.

I lean into his kiss and forget all about the fact that we still haven't talked about the future.

20

Sarah

As I flip pancakes for our breakfast with Jenni and Niko, my mind is fifteen miles away.

I have a meeting later this morning with a potential buyer who is looking for an RV to take south for the winter. It's the first bite I've had, and I'm hoping we are both desperate enough to make a same-day decision. I'm also scared to death that this could be a scam, or that I will mess it up somehow.

"Jenni just texted they're here," Piper says from where she's making eggs on the other side of the kitchen.

"Why don't you go let them in. I'll take the food to the dining room," I tell her. She kisses me on her way out of the kitchen, and a bolt of electricity flies through my body. It's funny how that still happens, even after so much time together.

Now that Piper is gone, I check my email to confirm the meeting about the RV is still on. I'm supposed to meet the guy at 11 a.m. I was nervous to tell Piper that I was going to my parents' house for a few hours today, but she had some errands to run and didn't need my help anyway. She wouldn't tell me the kind of errands, just that it was a few things for the inn and that she could handle it. I wish she wouldn't put so much on herself.

That's why I need to propose, so that she knows we're in this together. Always.

I take our food through the kitchen doors into the dining room as Piper, Jenni, and Niko enter through the French doors on the other side of the room.

"That smells amazing," Niko says.

"Thank you," I reply. "I'm sure it's nothing like the five-star restaurant at the Omorfiá, but welcome to our little dining room."

"Are you kidding me?" he asks. "This room is great. It's so cozy, and the whole ambiance promises a delicious home-cooked meal."

I can see why Jenni fell for him. Niko can see the good in every situation.

"That's the vibe we're going for," Piper says, pulling out a chair.

"Then you're doing something right," Jenni chimes in. She helps me move the plates of food to the table, along with maple syrup, a berry compote, and salt and pepper for the eggs.

"I'm sorry we don't have any bacon," I say. "I burned it. I'm still getting used to our new stovetop griddle."

Truthfully, I got distracted thinking about creating a chalkboard menu for the dining room. I could doodle each menu item using cute themes and colors. It would evoke European café vibes. I don't say the idea out loud, though, for fear of more eye-rolling at my daydreaming.

We all sit and dig in. The pancakes are fluffy and warm, perfect with melted butter and compote. Niko digs into the eggs, which Piper scrambled with sharp cheddar and fresh chives. The aroma is divine, even if I don't really like eggs. "So what's on the agenda today for our favorite inn owners?" Niko asks.

"I've got some last-minute errands to run for the inn." Piper takes another bite of the pancakes before continuing. "Actually, Jenni, do you and Niko have some time to help me with a few things today? I need some more muscle."

I look at Piper, confused. She told me she didn't need any help when I offered earlier. But apparently, she didn't want *my* help. I can't blame her. She's probably worried that I'll add more to her plate with all of my silly ideas.

"Yeah, of course. Put us to work," Jenni says. Niko nods in agreement between bites.

I take a sip of my coffee. I might need some help this afternoon, too. Someone a lot more experienced with finances than I am. Someone like Niko. "Wait, that's not fair that you get both of them," I say to Piper, trying to sound casual and playful. "You can have Jenni, but I'm taking Niko to my parents' house."

The three of them look at me, surprised.

"What?" I ask. "It will give me a chance to get to know him better. I promise to be nice."

I direct that last part at Jenni, who I'm sure is worried I might tell Niko some stories about her. I want to say, *trust me, your teen years are the last thing on my mind right now.*

"Sure, sounds great," Niko says. Little does he know what he's about to walk into.

ONCE NIKO IS in my car and Piper and Jenni have left in the truck, I confess. "I lured you here under false pretenses."

Niko looks up, surprised. "So, we're not going to your parents' house?"

"We are," I say. "But not to help them with anything. We are going to meet a potential buyer for our RV. I need to sell it, and I thought it might help to have you with me. Since you're, you know ..."

"I'm what?"

"Well, a man for one. Not Black for two. And good with money for three."

Niko laughs. "It sounds like you're setting up a racist dating profile, rather than selling a vehicle."

"Sorry," I say, my voice strained. "I just *really* can't mess this up."

"Okay, I get it," Niko responds. "But why don't you just bring Piper? I'm sure the two of you could handle it together."

I pause while waiting to turn left at an intersection. My blinker fills the silence. "I haven't told her I am selling it."

I hold my breath, waiting for Niko to scold me about keeping major decisions a secret from my girlfriend. Instead, he meets me with an open mind. "And I assume you have a good reason for not looping her in?"

I keep my eyes on the road, but I can see Niko out of my periphery, turning in his seat to face me. "Promise me you won't tell Piper. Or Jenni. The two of them share a telepathic connection, I swear."

"I promise," Niko says.

I take a deep breath. "I need money to buy an engagement ring."

I sneak a glance at Niko in the passenger seat. He's beaming. "That's incredible, Sarah. I'm so happy for the two of you."

Well, she hasn't said "yes" yet, but I appreciate his confidence that she will. "Thanks, me too." I can't stop a smile from spreading across my face.

Niko rubs the back of his neck with his hand. "Can I tell you a secret?"

"Sure," I say, as I pull onto the highway. "I'll use it for leverage."

He takes a deep breath. "I'm not going back to Mykonos."

His words hang between us in the heated air. "What do you mean you're not going back?"

"Not at all. I quit my job and packed all my clothes."

"What are you going to do instead?" As soon as I ask the question, realization strikes. "Oh, my God! You're moving here? To be with Jenni?"

He chuckles. "Ding, ding, ding."

"She's going to be so happy," I say, squealing like a schoolgirl. I'm regretting our sworn secrecy, because this might kill me. It's such a huge romantic gesture. And Jenni has been so worried. She deserves a big show of love and support; no one has ever put that much effort in for her before. "When are you going to tell her?"

"Christmas morning, hopefully, if I can wait that long. She keeps trying to make plans to come visit me, and I can only put her off so many times before she starts asking questions."

I'm taken aback. That's probably the worst way for him to handle this. No wonder her insecurities are off the charts. "Don't wait. She doesn't do well with uncertainty. She could spook."

"That's what I'm afraid of," he says. "With her past, I try always to be upfront. But this is the only gift I could give her that would come close to showing her how much I care. I have to hide it for one more week."

When we pull up to my parents' property, we barely wait five minutes before a man in a flashy truck pulls in behind us. The kind of truck one drives for style, rather than hauling loads. When he gets out, my heart pounds out of my chest. I don't know if I'm going to survive this. My hands are sweaty, and I feel panicky.

The man is wearing a knee-length wool coat and leather boots that belong in New York City, not the mountains of Colorado. This is not a man familiar with life on the road, which makes me nervous that the RV will be a hard sell.

"Hi, I'm Mitchell," he says. "I assume you're Sarah." He looks me over, and then Niko. "And you are?"

"Just a friend," Niko says. A part of me was hoping he would take over the deal for me—no such luck.

"The RV is right around here," I say to Mitchell, gesturing to the side of the garage. "She's fully up to date on all mainte-nance and runs like a well-oiled machine. She's already been winterized, but I'm happy to show the maintenance records and papers."

"What about any water damage? Smoking in the vehicle? Pets?" I can't help but notice the look he makes when he says RV, as if he's disgusted by the fact that I referred to it with pronouns. Seems like a fun guy. Niko sneaks an eye roll behind his back, but I'm too nervous to see the humor.

"No smoking, no pets, and definitely no water damage," I say with a smile. I make eye contact with Niko. I want to ask, *am I doing okay?*

"And what about the paint on the cupboards?"

My landscapes? I have so many memories of painting while Piper worked late into the night. "Yes! All original and hand-painted. I did them myself while we traveled the U.S."

"Acrylic or oil-based?" He's so blunt, I almost think I must have misheard him. Surely, he's not the type to be interested in the type of paint I used.

"Excuse me?"

"Is it oil-based or will it clean off easily?"

My stomach twists in knots. Is he saying he wants to erase

the one thing that makes our RV stand out in a crowd? I look at Niko, who stands stoically, waiting for me to speak.

"You want to … get rid of the paintings?"

"Yes," Mitchell says, with zero empathy. "They're not really my style."

I'm starting to wonder how this man's style is remotely compatible with RV life at all. Is he planning to drive it to Silicon Valley and live out his dream of becoming a venture capitalist? It just doesn't make sense.

"Can I ask what your plans are for the RV?"

He looks like he is already bored with our conversation. "My girlfriend wants to go on some camping trips next summer. It makes sense to invest in a vehicle that we can rent out later than renting one ourselves."

Oh, I see. He's only in this for the money. He doesn't care about the RV at all; he only sees a business opportunity. Embarrassment prickles my cheeks.

I can't sell to this guy. He wants to turn the RV into a paycheck. Our RV is too special for that. It was our home. I'm starting to feel out of breath, thinking about all the times I've been told my art doesn't matter by my parents, teachers, and employers who told me to fall in line and do the sensible thing.

Niko walks over and opens the door to the RV. "Mitchell, why don't you take a look inside while Sarah and I have a chat?"

The man grunts but heads inside. Niko pulls me a few yards away. "What's going on?"

"I can't sell our home to someone who just wants to use it as an *investment*. He doesn't care at all." I think that's what hurts the most. He didn't even want to look at it. That's how detached he is.

"I get that," Niko says. "It feels like you're selling a piece of yourself, but you can't look at it that way. You have no control over what happens to the RV once it leaves your possession.

Even an enthusiastic outdoorsman could crash it tomorrow, or change jobs and abandon it at a storage facility."

He's right. Anything could happen. I didn't think I would have to hear about it. I hold my breath. Handing over the RV feels like parting from a family member. I want to be able to trust the person who brings her home.

"Is the future you want with Piper worth letting go of the future of the RV?" Niko asks.

I picture that perfect ring at the mall and Piper. I would sacrifice everything for her, and my body relaxes. The answer is crystal clear. This might be my only chance to sell the RV at the right price before Christmas. That's the only way I can responsibly purchase that ring. It's a worthwhile sacrifice.

I look at Niko and give a slight nod, grateful that he's here. I turn around as Mitchell is stepping down out of the RV.

"The paint is acrylic," I tell him, my voice steady. "It can be cleaned off with warm, soapy water and a scraper. This will make a great rental RV. It's easy to operate and very reliable."

"Consider it purchased then. I'll wire you the money. Can you hold it here until I arrange storage?"

"Sure," I say. "Just call me when you're ready to collect it."

He nods and walks back to his car, taking a phone call before he even reaches the cab of his truck.

As Mitchell drives away, he takes a piece of my heart with him that I know he won't protect. My love for Piper will fill the gap left behind.

"You okay?" Niko asks.

"I am," I say. "Or I will be. Do you have time to run to the jewelry store with me?"

21

Piper

Today's the first day that the lake is open for ice skating.

This was always my favorite day of the winter season growing up. The whole town comes together to ice skate on the lake. Food trucks line the road and bonfires dot the shoreline. Jenni and I used to go every year, but when Sarah joined the picture in our last two years of high school, we stopped. Maybe we thought we were too cool for the cozy, small-town event. We were probably off in Golden or Denver, trying to prove how independent and grown up we were. *Such teenagers.*

Tonight, however, I can't wait to embrace all of it, from supporting the local businesses to seeing everyone I've been trying to hide from for the last few months. If I want to stake our claim in this community, events like this are how it happens. And I'm going to enjoy it.

"I can't wait for you to experience this," I tell Sarah. "It's straight out of a Christmas movie. Skating on the lake beneath market lights and a star-filled sky."

She smiles at me and leans in for a kiss. "Just don't let me fall on my face. I think I've been skating once in my entire life."

My heart swells with the assignment. I will be the best skate partner on the ice—never without an arm around her. "I wouldn't dream of it."

"Good. Can you also promise not to worry about the inn for just a few hours? Pretty please!" Her large, brown eyes are filled with a childlike hope.

"I'm going to try," I say earnestly. "I want to have fun tonight, for once."

When Niko and Jenni arrive, the four of us head to the rental shack to suit up. "Are you two ready for this?" I ask, directing the question at Sarah and Niko. "Because Jenni and I are basically Olympians when it comes to Pineview Lake."

Niko looks around at people of all ages on the ice. "We'll survive," he says decisively with a conspiratorial look at Sarah.

As soon as the four of us step out onto the ice, I barely make it three strides before a man stops me. He used to work for my dad at the adventure company. "Piper, it's good to see you! I heard you were back in town. How are things going at the inn?"

In the last couple of weeks, I have come to hate that question more than anything. I never have the answer that I want, which is that everything is perfect. But it's nice to finally feel like it's a friendly face asking the question, instead of someone with ulterior motives.

"It's going well. I'm just getting all the last pieces together. Will you be joining us in a few days?"

"Of course, I'm bringing the whole family," he says. "Will your parents come up from Texas?"

"No, they'll be here in a few weeks, though. They're spending the holidays with my grandma."

"Tell your dad to stop by and say hello, okay? I'd love to see him."

"I will," I say. That will make Dad happy.

"Can't wait to see you at the opening," Sarah chimes in. She takes my hand and whispers in my ear as we skate away. "See? That wasn't so bad. There are a lot of people who want to support you."

"I know, I just ... don't want to disappoint them."

"We won't."

I squeeze her hand, and we try to catch up to Jenni and Niko. As soon as we reach them, Niko spins out of control, his legs flying in opposite directions. In a second, he pulls Jenni down with him, and we're headed for a roadblock. I twist my body, turning my skates sideways to stop, but Sarah panics and tries to veer around our friends who are now piled on the ice.

Sarah has my hand in a death grip, so when I stop and she keeps moving, the momentum sends her skates flying up into the air, and she lands on her butt right next to Jenni and Niko. I'm left towering over the three of them.

"Are you all okay?" I say, my heart racing with adrenaline. I can't believe I let Sarah fall. It all happened so fast, I couldn't stop it. Sarah is gasping and grabbing her hip. She's hurt.

I drop to my knees on the ice, checking her over. "Sarah, what's wrong?"

All three of them are squirming and gasping for air as if they fell through the ice into the frigid water. I don't know who to check on first. And then I realize, they are laughing. All of them. They are heaving in laughter, barely making any noise. "You guys! I was freaking out!"

"Sorry," Niko says, rolling over onto his hands and knees. "That was my fault. I tried to be fancy and ended up taking everyone down with me."

I stand, steadying myself on the ice before pulling him to

his feet. We each help our partners to stand, giggling the entire time.

"You should have seen your face," Sarah tells me. "That's what had me laughing. You looked like you had witnessed a car crash, not an ice-skating mishap."

My cheeks flush. "It was pretty catastrophic. You didn't see it."

"Don't worry. We know it's just because you care so much," Jenni says, wrapping her arm around my shoulder and giving me a squeeze. "Now, let's show them how it's done."

"You're on," I say.

Jenni and I race a lap at full speed, leaving Niko and Sarah to struggle together. We circle around to join them. They've only traveled about ten feet from where we left them.

"You ready to try again?" I ask, putting my hands on Sarah's hips and gently gliding behind her to keep her steady.

"Yes, but I think we should be in front this time," she jokes. We take our place in the lead and make our way around the ice. *Life is good.*

An hour later, everyone's ankles are tired, so we retire our skates and head for the food stalls. "What sounds good to everyone?" I ask, as we survey the offerings: bratwurst, candied apples, hot chocolate, funnel cakes.

"Oh, that one," Jenni cries in excitement and drags the group to a stall selling Palisade Peach Crisp.

As soon as we get in line, the sweet smell of peaches fills my nose, and I can see why Jenni insisted on eating here.

"Okay, Niko, remember when you fed me the apricot in Greece, and I didn't know apricots could taste that good?"

"I do," he answers.

"Well, that's about to happen to you with peaches," Jenni continues. "Western Colorado, especially an area called Palisade, is famous for their peaches. They are the biggest, juiciest, sweetest peaches you'll ever have."

"But these probably aren't fresh," Sarah says. "The peaches are harvested in early fall."

"No, I'm sure they freeze them," Jenni says and turns to Niko. "But it will still be the best peach crisp you've ever had."

"I'm drooling just smelling it," Niko says.

"The peaches are best when you get them straight off a truck driving from the farms in Palisade. We used to buy them by the crate," I tell the group.

"So true," Jenni and Sarah say in unison, moaning.

We get to the front of the line, and Jenni orders four crisp packets. Behind the stand, a dozen foil packets sit on a stainless steel grate over hot coals. The food worker grabs a packet with grill tongs and drops it into a paper serving tray.

Once he has four ready to go, he slices open the foil packets with giant scissors, dumps a scoop of vanilla ice cream on top, and finally adds a spoon. Jenni takes them and passes them out to us one at a time. The hot crisp warms my hands.

We take our food to an open steel drum bonfire along the shore of the frozen lake, and I take my first, steamy bite of the dessert. The sweet taste of peaches mixed with brown sugar, butter, and oats warms my insides. It tastes like childhood.

Niko holds up his spoon, dripping with gooey syrup that looks like molten amber. "This is amazing. I think you've ruined any other fruity dessert for the rest of my life."

"That good, huh?" Jenni says, smiling. I know how much it means to her that he enjoys his time here, and I think we've just sealed the deal. Jenni starts to say more, but then stops suddenly. "Sarah? Is everything okay?"

We all turn to my girlfriend, who is staring at her phone with a queasy look on her face. "Babe, what's wrong?"

"I just got an email. The shipment is delayed. The comforters aren't going to get here in time."

The bonfire crackles in the silence between us. The

company had promised us two-day shipping. Which meant they should have arrived by now. How is this possible?

"When are they going to get here?" Jenni asks, finally.

I'm glad she asked it because I can't make words come out of my mouth right now. We're past the point where we can still fix this. There is no way. We won't be able to open unless we want our guests to use old sleeping bags.

The peaches turn acidic in my stomach.

"January tenth," Sarah says in a whisper. Her face is made of stone.

"*What?*" I finally say. "That's almost a month later. How is that possible?"

Sarah shows me her phone, and I skim the email. A flood at the warehouse halted their entire operation, leaving them unable to use any of the fabrics or products they had already manufactured. They don't think they'll be able to get everything back up and running until after Christmas.

My chest tightens with each word I read. "We're doomed. We are opening in six days."

Sarah looks equally in shock. We stare at each other, unsure of what to do. I look to Jenni and Niko.

"All right, let's get back to the inn. We can problem-solve there," Niko says.

"Yeah, we'll figure this out," Jenni adds, grabbing my hand. "It will be okay."

The walk back to the car is a nauseous blur. Somehow, I navigate the truck back to the inn. Sarah keeps apologizing, but I don't know what to say. I'm silent for the entire drive.

We're sitting around one of the dining room tables, racking our brains on how to possibly fix this. Niko has been on the phone, calling other manufacturers. He hasn't gotten anything other than voicemails or, worse, a recorded message telling him to call back in January.

Jenni and Sarah have been scouring the internet for in-store options down in Denver. I'm desperate enough now to put superhero bedspreads on all of the beds. As long as they'll keep our guests warm, I don't care what they look like.

"I'm so sorry. This is all my fault," Sarah says with tears coursing down her cheeks. "I should have listened to you and gone with the standard option. We never would have had so many problems."

My chest feels hot with the desire to say something I'll regret later. I resist the urge and grab her hand across the table instead. "Don't blame yourself. We both made choices we can't take back. What's important now is finding a solution."

Jenni's phone rings, and she quickly gets up and walks out to the lobby.

Sarah blows her nose with a tissue. "Piper, how can you say that? I was the one who insisted on having character. I'm the one who said white would be boring. I'm so sorry."

I put my face in my hands rather than answer her. I don't know what to say. I don't know how to fix this so that she doesn't have to feel responsible. I hate that I can't protect her from this guilt.

"Worst case scenario, we drive to the nearest department store and buy up whatever we can find," I say. "They don't have to match or be perfect. We just need blankets. The color and style don't matter at this point."

Her body tenses with resistance. I know that's the worst thing I could have said to an artistic mind like hers, but it's the truth.

A knock sounds at the open French doors that Jenni just walked out of. I look up, expecting to see her returning from her phone call. I gasp when I see Patty, Kathy, and half a dozen other women from the knitting club, including Linda LeGrande, all holding plastic tubs.

"We heard there was a blanket emergency?" Kathy asks, a massive grin on her face.

"I … yeah. What is this? What are you doing here?" I ask, confused.

"Kathy saw the four of you abandon your food at the lake and walk like zombies to the parking lot. We sent Jenni a text message to see if everything was okay, and she filled us in," Patty explains. "We know you like your privacy, but what is the point of living in a small town if you can't rely on your friends to help you out?"

A warm fire crackles to life inside my chest. They came. They heard I needed help, and they came to my aid. "I don't know what to say."

"Just point us to the rooms," Linda says. I still can't believe she, of all people, is standing here in my inn, lending me a hand. "We've brought all of our unused quilts and knitted blankets. Most of these were made for the state fair or quilt shows. They are all very high quality if I do say so myself. Better than you could find at any store."

She preens and winks at the women surrounding her.

My jaw drops. "You brought blankets?"

"Yes, from the whole group," Patty says. "We got a little concerned the last time we were here that you weren't telling us the whole bedding situation, so we pulled all of this together just in case."

"You—" I choke on my words, a knot of emotion swelling in my throat. I put a hand over my mouth.

"I think what she means is thank you," Sarah says for me. "From the bottom of our hearts. You're literally saving us."

"We mountain folk have to stick together," Kathy says with a laugh, looking around the room. "No matter what anyone says, you girls are part of our Pineview Springs family."

The group spreads out to each guest room, making the beds with these gifted quilts.

Each blanket is unique and more beautiful than the last, featuring mountains, stars, black bears, and pine trees. Some are textured waffle knit or cable knit, while others are quilted from the most beautiful cotton and backed with flannel. These blankets feel more right than anything else we could have possibly found.

"It's like a piece of the town in every room," Sarah states after we make the final bed. "It's perfect. Exactly the way I envisioned it."

I will never complain about nosy knitting ladies, ever again. They have saved us.

We offer everyone coffee for their troubles, but most refuse, telling us to get some rest.

After everyone leaves for the night, Sarah and I retreat to our room, and I can't help but feel a boulder-sized weight lifted off my shoulders as we settle in.

22

Niko

PINEVIEW SPRINGS, COLORADO
TWO DAYS BEFORE OPENING

As Jenni and I approach her parents' front door, I'm more nervous than I think I've ever been in my life. We're having dinner with Jenni's family, and if I'm going to move here and be in their lives for the foreseeable future, I want to make a good first impression.

"Are you ready?" Jenni asks me outside the front door.

"Of course, let's do it," I respond. I should probably tell her that I'm nervous, but I hate admitting things like that. She has always seen me as self-assured. She once told me my confidence was the first thing she noticed about me. So how can I show any hesitation, now? I don't want her to think it means that I'm unsure of her.

Jenni opens the door, and we walk in. "We're here!" she calls.

We head toward the kitchen and find her mom at the stove

while her dad and brother sit at the kitchen table. They both stand to greet us.

Jenni's dad hugs her and then shakes my hand. Jeremy hugs us both.

"How was your flight?" I ask.

"Not bad," Jeremy says.

"That's because you were asleep," Jenni's mom says, wiping her hands on her apron and hugging Jenni. "There was a ton of turbulence for those of us who stayed awake. I was a nervous wreck."

Jenni catches my eye over her mom's shoulder, and I can tell she's holding back a laugh. "I'm glad you made it back safely."

"Me too, honey," she tells Jenni and then moves in for a hug with me. "Niko, it is so great to meet you."

"Thank you for having me, Mrs. Swanson," I tell her. "I'm so happy to be here."

"Oh, call me Rebecca," she says, and then gestures to her husband. "And call him Tim. None of this formal nonsense."

"Sounds good, Rebecca," I say, making sure I do what she says. "Can we help with dinner at all?"

She turns to survey the kitchen, considering my offer. "If you want to slice the garlic bread, I won't complain."

Jenni and I head to the steaming loaf of garlic bread on the counter. Jenni grabs a bread knife and hands it over. I slice, while she retrieves a basket and lines it with a paper napkin. Once all of the food is ready, we head into the dining room and sit at the table.

Rebecca sets down a pan of aromatic lasagna, smelling of oregano and tomato. And Tim brings over a large salad bowl and the bread basket. We all serve ourselves from the middle of the table, and I try to remember the last time I sat down for a home-cooked family meal.

My mom wasn't much of a cook, and it was just the two of

us. My grandma cooked when I visited her in the summers, though, and it's one of my favorite memories growing up.

"Niko, Jenni tells me you grew up in California, but now you're in Greece?" Jeremy asks.

I clear my throat. "Yes, it's a long story, but my parents are both Greek, and they grew up together in the same social circles. My mom's family is in the oil industry, and she always resented being raised as a socialite without the opportunity to pursue her own interests. She wanted to move to the States, but my dad was taking over his dad's winery and wanted to stay in Greece, so they split up, and I was born in California."

I take a sip of water and realize that the story has impacted the family more than I expected. Rebecca is holding her fork halfway to her mouth, frozen, with eyes wide. "It was really amicable. They just wanted different things. Neither one ever remarried, so it's just been me and my mom, and we visited Greece every year."

"Sounds awesome to me," Jeremy says. "I'd love to visit sometime. Your hotel is in Mykonos, right?"

"Jeremy," Jenni chastises him. "You can't just invite yourself to his hotel." She blushes, looking uncomfortable.

Ever since Breckenridge, Jenni has been weird whenever we mention the future, probably because I changed the subject every single time. I regret my plan to delay talks about moving, because it has really affected her. I want to make plans, of course. But they are different from the plans she's thinking about.

I want to make plans for an apartment and regular Sunday dinners, not months without seeing each other. When she's brought it up, I've changed the subject or put off the conversation. Over the last few days, though, she has stopped bringing up anything past Christmas. It's like she expects the relationship to end at that point. I'm worried that I've messed up.

Hopefully, once everything is in the open and she knows I'm not going back to Greece, she'll forgive me.

"Your mom must have had a hard time with your decision to move to Greece," Rebecca says, sounding like she's speaking from experience. Jenni told me her mom was ecstatic when Jenni moved back home from Chicago.

"She misses me," I tell her, trying to be sympathetic to her perspective. "I don't think she really understands my choices, but she does her best to be supportive."

That's another reason I'm excited to move back. My mom will be thrilled. She has a vast social network, but very little family here. I take a bite of my lasagna, ready to be done talking about myself.

"Niko has completely revolutionized the Omorfiá," Jenni says.

"Revolutionized is a strong word," I laugh. "I have implemented a few unconventional changes, focusing on community involvement rather than solely tourism, and it has paid off. Actually, it was Jenni who helped me see that my ideas were worthwhile."

I grab my glass as Jenni starts to object, but her dad speaks first. "We've heard some of the things you're doing," he says. "What are you doing next?"

I choke on my water. It's a simple enough question. I should have prepared an elevator pitch about the future of the hotel, but I haven't thought about it once since the afternoon I had Ana in my office.

"Nothing concrete," I say. "My cousin is in charge of the hotel's event planning and community outreach. She probably has a dozen ideas she hasn't told me about yet."

Not that she needs to tell me anymore. The thought makes me smile. She's going to do great things.

"Jeremy, how did you get into video game design?" I ask,

shifting the topic of conversation away from myself and the hotel.

"I always loved games growing up. Card games, board games, video games, you name it," he says. "Then in high school, I took a multimedia class and created a basic RPG game that involved pirates and mermaids. The graphics were terrible, but I fell in love with the concept of game design and theory."

"Within a year, he had taken every graphic design class he could at the community college down the mountain," Jenni adds, beaming with pride. "He put an indie game on the market before he even graduated."

"I sold the game to a company in Seattle and then went to work for them when I graduated," Jeremy says, as if it were the most normal thing in the world to skip college and go straight into a career.

"We can still beat him in Uno, though," Tim says. "Should we have a game after dinner?"

"Yes! You'll love it," Jenni says to me. Then turns to the rest of the table. "Do we still have the poster of our Uno house rules?"

"I think so," Rebecca says, a glimmer in her eye. "I believe it's in the den. We can check after dinner."

Thirty minutes later, Jeremy has just played a Draw Four card to Jenni. Instead of drawing from the pile, however, she says, "Hit me with the trivia."

Tim pulls out a small box of handwritten flash cards. "When the kids were young, I would write new trivia cards every week, depending on what they were learning at school," Tim explains. "If they answered correctly, they could get out of drawing extra Uno cards."

"Once a teacher, always a teacher," Rebecca chimes in. "But it certainly made studying more fun, right?"

Jeremy and Jenni both agree.

"Niko, would you do the honors of reading the card?" Tim asks, handing me the first flashcard in the box.

I take it. "In what year did the moon landing occur?" I ask.

"Oh, that's way too easy," Jeremy gripes. Jenni, however, looks blank-faced.

"I know it was in the sixties," she says. "But I have no idea which year."

"You have to give an answer," Tim instructs. "Even if you're just guessing."

"1965..." She says, wincing.

"Wrong," Jeremy says, immediately. "1969. Draw four and cry to Mommy."

"Jeremy," Rebecca scolds, but everyone else is laughing, including Jenni.

"It's okay, Mom, that's what Swanson Uno is all about," Jenni tells Rebecca. "Your turn, Niko."

I play a skip card, and the game moves straight past Tim and onto Rebecca. She plays a reverse card, and everyone except me jumps up and spins around. "Come on, Niko, you have to do the reverse dance," Rebecca calls out. I get to my feet and spin around twice. My heart jumps.

This is incredible. Growing up with just my mom, we didn't have game nights. We visited museums and talked about art and food, but never with this type of rambunctious play.

I can tell how much the Swansons enjoy each other's company. It's precisely the type of family atmosphere I always dreamed about.

After three rounds of Uno, we're all laughing so hard that tears glisten in our eyes, and we decide to call it quits.

"Okay, Jenni," Jeremy says. "Niko kept up with Swanson Uno. You can keep him."

She blushes redder than a Santa suit.

"Phew," I say, wiping my brow. "I was nervous I wouldn't make the cut." I lean down and kiss the top of her head.

"I almost forgot we have eggnog," Rebecca says, getting to her feet while the rest of us clean up the cards. "Should we take it to the living room?"

"Sounds great," Tim says.

"Brandy or no brandy?" Rebecca asks.

In unison, the siblings both respond, "Brandy!"

We all settle on the couches in the living room, and Tim starts a fire. The crackling of the fire brings the room to life as we sip our eggnog.

"How long are you in town, Niko? Will we get to have you over again?" Rebecca asks.

I look over at Jenni, an unreadable look on her face. "I'll be in Colorado until the twenty-eighth, and then Jenni and I will visit my mom in California for New Year's."

I take another sip and put my arm around Jenni.

"And then he'll go back to Mykonos," she adds with a note of finality.

"I guess someone has to run the hotel," Tim says. "I'm surprised you've been able to take this much time off already."

I shrug, trying to play it off. "This is our quietest time of year, thankfully."

"That's good," Rebecca says. "Jenni will surely miss you when you go back."

I squeeze Jenni to my side, but she continues her silence.

"I will miss her, too," I say, knowing it's a complete fabrication. I won't need to miss her. I refuse to commit full PDA in front of Jenni's family, even though I want to pull her in for a passionate, reassuring kiss. Instead, I turn her face toward mine and try to convey the same emotions with my eyes.

She smiles up at me, but a hint of sadness lingers in her expression. *Just wait a few more days,* I want to tell her.

23

Sarah

The butter and sugar mixture bubbles and churns as it heats, filling the inn's kitchen with a warm, caramel-like aroma. It has almost the perfect temperature for making fudge, so while I stir, I pull the bowl of chocolate chips and marshmallow fluff closer, ready to go. Once it reaches the temperature I need, I'll add the final ingredients quickly and stir until my arm falls off. If I waste any time, the fudge might come out streaky or clumpy, rather than creamy.

A few minutes ago, Piper's truck pulled in and drove back to our storage sheds. I wish I could help her with whatever she's unloading, but I can't burn my grandma's award-winning fudge that we are serving at the grand opening tomorrow night.

We've spent the entire day getting ready for tomorrow, and it's now after dinner. Our cleaning crew was here earlier, sprucing up all of the guest rooms, cleaning the bathrooms, and dusting every square inch of the inn. The kitchen staff filled the pantry and prepped food for tomorrow. And Piper and I set up outside for the party.

Tomorrow, we'll open for check-ins in the afternoon and then invite the guests and community to join us on the patio a few hours later. I've coordinated with a local brewery to provide drinks and a DJ for music at the gathering. Piper has set up fire pits, bar-height wooden tables, and outdoor heaters. Everything is finally coming together.

Including my fudge. I already have three pans sitting on the counter, and once this batch is done and set, I'll cut the fudge into squares, wrap them individually in plastic wrap, and affix a Pineview Inn sticker to each. Nothing says Christmas to me like Grandma's fudge, and I couldn't imagine the grand opening without it.

Piper arrives in the kitchen just as I finish pouring the last of the fudge.

"Hey! Welcome home," I say to Piper. "What were you up to? You never told me."

"Oh, nothing, just collecting some extra firewood for tomorrow and making sure we have everything we need."

We have both been feeling on cloud nine since the knitting group showed up to the rescue. We tried to pay them, but they wouldn't accept it. So instead, we offered them all a complimentary night's stay this spring. I think they're all going to book the same weekend for a "quilt-in." It turns out they do more than knit. They sew, quilt, and embroider. I have overlooked their talent and creativity up until now. I always imagined them knitting potholders or cross-stitching scripture verses. I shouldn't have judged. I wonder if they'll accept a girl in her twenties into the group. I need more friends now that we're settling here.

"How's it looking out there?" I ask.

"Believe it or not, it is finally snowing. We may have a white Christmas. Or at least a white opening."

"Oh, that will be magical!" I squeal. The inn will look like a winter wonderland under fresh snow with the lights, the wooden beams, and the roasting fires. Pure winter enchantment.

"I know," Piper says. "But I should probably go get more salt and maybe some ice scrapers for the guests in case they don't bring any with them. Hopefully I'll run into Charlie at the hardware store and ask him about that Christmas wildfire he was predicting."

"What are you talking about?" I ask, putting foil over the fudge while it cools and sets.

"Oh, nothing," Piper says. "I forgot I hadn't told you about that. I had a run-in with him a few weeks ago that sent me spiraling for a while, but I'm doing better now."

That explains a lot. I wish I had known so I could have helped her. "Are you sure you're okay now? What did he say?"

"He was just upset about past grievances. The knitting group showed me the other night that even though Charlie has a loud voice, it's not the only voice that matters. We have the community at our back, and tomorrow is going to show it."

"I'm so happy to hear that," I say. "I've been worried about you."

"All better now," Piper tells me. "Just a blip in the road."

She leans in for a kiss and then grabs her keys from the counter.

"Don't stay out too long. Jenni and Niko are on their way over," I remind her. "We're going to put together the s'mores kits for tomorrow."

"Perfect, I'll be back in an hour or so." She kisses me on the cheek before heading back out to her truck.

Niko and Jenni knock on the kitchen door as I'm dumping the bags of marshmallows, bars of chocolate, and boxes of graham crackers on one of the dining room tables. After a call from Niko, a company in Boulder donated 250 compostable baggies for the s'mores kits. He really has a knack for sustainability moves. I am going to make him give me more ideas for the inn, since he'll be staying around. The secret has been eating me up inside, but I keep quiet, knowing that in a few short days, Jenni will have her happy-ever-after.

As soon as I open the door to let them in, a gust of wind sends a flurry of snow into the kitchen. My friends hurry in, and I slam the door behind them. "Wow, it's really coming down out there," I observe.

"It's starting to stick, too," Jenni responds, smiling from ear to ear.

"I just hope it settles down a bit," I say. "We don't need a blizzard for opening day."

The three of us sit down and establish an assembly line of chocolate bars, graham crackers, and marshmallows.

When Piper comes home forty-five minutes later, I'm just tying a ribbon onto the last baggie. When I greet her at the door, snow is coming down hard and heavy.

"I could barely see the road," she says.

We all check our phones at the same time after they ping with a weather alert. Winter storm warnings have been issued for the entire Front Range. This storm is getting out of hand.

"This wasn't predicted, was it?" I ask the group. "Last I saw, we were only supposed to get an inch or two."

Jenni nods in agreement. "I had no idea. Piper, do you think Niko and I can drive home in this?"

"I wouldn't risk it," Piper says. "Why don't you stay here with us? We can check you into your room early."

We all take a moment to digest this new development. "It could be fun," I say, finally breaking the silence. "We could clean up in here and then play some games in the lodge room before turning in."

Niko is scrolling on his phone. "My weather app says it will still be snowing for a few hours, but it should stop sometime after midnight." Putting a hand on Jenni's back, he says, "Let's take them up on their offer. We can get the rest of our things tomorrow."

"It's settled then," she responds. "It's our first night at the inn!"

After putting the s'mores kits into baskets for tomorrow, the four of us take cups of winter spice tea to the lodge room, where we watch the snow fall through floor-to-ceiling windows. The room is small, but we've filled it with a table, four winged armchairs, and a small craft cart stocked with games, cards, and puzzles. The best part about the lodge room is the wood-burning fireplace on the far wall.

Piper grabs some logs and starts the fire. It crackles to life, filling the room with heat and a soft, cozy background noise.

"Should we start a puzzle? Guests can work on whatever we don't finish," I suggest. I love the thought of our guests wandering into the lodge room and adding a piece or two to the puzzle before going on their way. In no time, we'll have a completed puzzle that belongs to all of us.

Niko surveys a stack in the corner and grabs a puzzle of Rocky Mountain National Park featuring a herd of elk grazing near a lake. "How about this one?"

"Let's do it," Piper says.

We start by sorting the pieces into corners, edges, and middles. Piper and Jenni rush through, barely looking at the pieces before tossing them into their respective pile. Niko and I are both slower, inspecting each piece for its art and not just its shape.

After a while, we have everything sorted and start working on the edges.

Niko places a piece of the lake along the left-hand edge of

the puzzle. "Sarah, Jenni tells me that you have some great ideas for the inn. I'd love to hear about them."

My face flushes. "No, I don't think I'll be doing any creative thinking for a while. That's how we ended up needing emergency bedding."

"That's not true," Piper says. "That was just bad luck. Go on, tell him about your ideas."

"Please," Jenni agrees. "I want to hear more, too!"

I take a deep breath.

I feel so stupid when I think about all of that now. Getting the inn open has been hard enough. I don't know why I ever thought we could have a petting zoo, nature art classes, or a bookshop. I hadn't considered how much work it would actually be. Just like my parents always said, my head is in the clouds.

"Gosh, I don't know. I'd love to turn some of the land into a space for weddings." That feels like one of the more level-headed ideas, safe for sharing.

Piper interrupts. "She has also suggested cooking classes with local chefs, art workshops, or even hosting a seasonal petting zoo for the kids."

"Nice," Niko says, smiling at me. "Those are all great ideas."

"Isn't she brilliant?" Jenni asks.

My throat constricts. "Well, we can't afford any of that right now. When the inn is running well and we don't have to stretch ourselves too thin, maybe we'll consider."

Piper squeezes my hand under the table. I don't know what she means by it, and it doesn't keep me from feeling deflated.

I wish I had focused more on the logistics of running the inn rather than the aesthetics. I was so focused on the guest experience that I ended up putting a ton of pressure on Piper to make it all happen. The past few weeks have been hard on both of us.

"So Jenni and Niko, when is the next rendezvous? Are you heading back to Greece soon, Jenni?" Piper asks, changing the subject. I don't dare glance at Niko, but I can sense him tensing out of the corner of my eye.

"Hopefully soon," Jenni responds, sounding a bit irritated. "We haven't been able to settle on anything yet." The way she says it, I would know something was up even if she hadn't told us about their conversation a few days ago. Niko *needs* to tell her about his plan soon because this is precisely what I was afraid would happen.

As if on cue, he clears his throat. "It's my fault. I just wanted to focus on this trip. Once we pull out calendars and schedules, it reminds me too much that we will be apart again."

Oh, that was a good line. Jenni seems to relax slightly before she replies.

"That's exactly why I *want* to make sure we have a time and place picked out. Otherwise, I don't think I'll be able to stand saying goodbye."

"I'm sorry," Niko responds. "We'll figure it out. Just not tonight, okay?"

Jenni's shoulders drop. "Yeah, okay."

We complete a quarter of the puzzle, but everyone is far more reserved than we were before sitting down. We are each stuck in our own little worlds as the snow continues to fall all around us.

24

Jenni

PINEVIEW SPRINGS, COLORADO
OPENING DAY

I wake early the next morning, and my eyes take a minute to adjust to the brightness of my surroundings. There's an eerie silence, and I'm confused for a moment.

Where am I?

Niko's hand is on my hip, and as I move closer to his warmth, I remember that we're at the inn. And it's opening day.

I pull myself out from under Niko's arm and go to the window. We forgot to pull the blackout shades closed last night because it was so dark during the storm. Only the sheer white curtains obscure my view now. I pull them back to reveal a total whiteout outside.

Snow drifts stand three and four feet high. My little Subaru is buried in the parking lot. And all of the trees and metal surfaces are coated in thick ice, glinting in the sun, but not melting. It's breathtaking.

My chest tightens for a different reason. With this much snow and ice, will the roads be open?

I rush back to my phone on the nightstand and pull up the Colorado Department of Transportation app. Red circles mark road closures. Red lines indicate stopped traffic. Red triangles alert to accidents or roadblocks.

No. This can't be happening.

I tap on the alerts page. The interstate from Denver to the mountains is shut at the tunnel due to black ice. It won't open for hours. The small state highway that connects the interstate to Pineview Springs is also closed due to snow accumulation, high winds, and icy conditions. The small state highways are rarely cleared immediately after a storm. All the snowplows and resources will be deployed to high-traffic areas, such as the interstate and larger towns and cities. The entrance to Pineview Springs could stay closed for days. We are, quite literally, unreachable.

As I text Piper and Sarah to check if they are awake, a news alert pops up at the top of my screen. The airport is completely shut down, and all flights are canceled. What the heck happened last night?

I open the news article. A Polar Vortex swooped in overnight, colder and windier than anyone predicted. All the snow that fell yesterday froze into solid ice overnight. Then more snow and ice fell on top of it. I haven't seen a storm like this in years.

"Niko," I say, gently shaking his shoulder. "We need to get up. We need to talk to Piper and Sarah."

A few minutes later, all four of us are in the kitchen, holding mugs of coffee and staring out the door to the driveway.

"What are we going to do?" Sarah asks.

"We have to cancel," Piper responds, sounding in a daze. "We can't hold the grand opening tonight. No one will be able to make it because of the snow."

The fire pits Piper put out yesterday are covered, and the tables look like tiny stools sticking only two feet above the accumulated snow.

The two of them look shell-shocked. I want to cry and scream at the same time. They have worked so hard for something entirely out of their control to ruin this day. And for once, I can't think of anything we can do to fix it.

"Here's what we're going to do," Niko says, a strong dose of authority in his voice. He's stepping into general manager mode, and I could not be more grateful. "Piper, call all of the guests, leave a message that you understand they will be unlikely to make it to the inn, but that you will hold all reservations for as long as anyone needs to arrive safely, and that you will issue credits or refunds for any nights that go unused."

Piper nods, grateful that someone else is taking charge.

"Sarah," Niko continues, "call the staff. Check in with everyone first to see if they need anything, then ask what day they can make it to work. We'll need that information to decide when to move the opening."

Sarah's eyes focus now that we have an action plan.

It's hot watching Niko manage everything like this. I knew he was good at his job, but I hadn't seen him in crisis mode. I like it.

"Jenni and I will make calls to the community and let everyone know that the opening won't be happening for a few days. Once word starts spreading, we'll update our social media pages and determine when we can reasonably reschedule. Is everyone good?"

The girls both nod again and move to start making calls. Niko and I head to the dining room. "Thank you," I tell him.

"I don't think we ever expected something like this to happen. Not on opening day, at least."

"Of course," Niko says, wiping his brow. Maybe he wasn't as cool and collected as he seemed. "We've never had a Polar Vortex at the Omorfiá, but I've had to create all sorts of contingency plans for emergencies. Someday I'll tell you about the time a water main broke and we didn't have running water for five days. That was a nightmare."

I laugh, imagining Alexander's dedication to alerting the guests. He would have felt personally responsible for making sure every last person had their needs met. I miss him. I miss Ana. I miss the Omorfiá.

"Niko, can we please talk about why you don't want me to visit you in Greece?"

He looks up at me, his eyes wide. "What? Why do you think that?"

"Because you won't talk to me about it," I say, my voice cracking. I bite my lip to settle myself. "I have missed you so much, and it's crushing my soul to think about saying goodbye without knowing when I'll see you again. I'm so confused. Don't you feel the same way?" I hold my breath, waiting for his response.

I hate this. I shouldn't feel so insecure and clingy when he hasn't done anything wrong. But I do, and it's so frustrating that I haven't grown out of this. I thought I wasn't that girl anymore who put all of her hopes and dreams into one person. I should be happy whether Niko is here or not.

A few weeks ago, an extended trip to Greece felt like the best choice in the world. It was a risk, but I was confident in the reward. I knew it would be worth it. But now? I can't figure out why Niko doesn't want to move forward past this visit. I feel like I've made a giant mistake.

"Of course, I want you to visit," he tells me. "I don't think I can put into words how lonely this winter has been. I haven't told you because I wanted to protect you from my issues. I didn't want you to feel bad for living your life. You have so much going for you here with your job, and putting all of this together with your best friends." He gestures at the inn. "I haven't wanted to get in the way of any of it."

So, we're both pretending to be okay because we didn't want to weigh the other person down? I don't know why I expected him to say anything different. Relief floods my veins when I realize what it means. He does want me to visit. He isn't trying to keep our lives separate; he is just trying to support me.

Before I can respond, Niko grabs my phone off the table. "I promise we will talk about it, but right now we have phone calls to make. Piper and Sarah need us."

He's right. I'm being selfish for even bringing this up right now when there are far bigger problems. When I tell him I'm coming to Greece in January, we can talk more about it. We are going to have to get better at communicating these feelings so we don't get stuck in this rut again, neither wanting to ask for too much and staying in quiet pain instead.

We sit next to each other at the table, our knees knocking as we start initiating the unofficial Pineview Springs phone tree.

For the next hour, I call everyone I can think of in town to let them know about the cancellation. Everyone is understanding. Plus, once we get in touch with the knitting group, I know the entire town will be aware of the situation within the next few hours.

Niko called the vendors for the grand opening and updated the inn's social media pages, encouraging the followers to spread the word.

When we're done, we head to the lobby to check on Piper and Sarah. They've wrapped up making all of their phone calls.

"How did it go?" I ask.

"Pretty good," Piper says, wiping her hands on her pajama pants. "Most of our guests are stuck in Denver, unable to make it up the mountain. The local guests agreed to wait until we can get everything cleaned up and have everyone check in at the same time."

"I'm sure they have things to take care of at their homes too," I say. "I'm glad everyone is being flexible."

"Most of the staff will be able to come in as soon as the roads open," Sarah adds. "A few are trying to figure out child-care options if their daycares don't reopen as early as we do. But we should be okay."

The two of them look exhausted. I keep thinking how unfair this is. How could this happen to them? They've worked so hard and been through so much to get this inn reopened. They don't deserve for it all to come crashing to a halt because of the weather.

"What do we do now?" Piper asks, and we all look at Niko.

"Don't ask me," he says. "My expertise ends at business logistics. Dealing with snow is not something I'm accustomed to. Do we wait it out? Start shoveling?"

I laugh.

"No, we can't do anything until the temperatures rise. Everything out there is ice right now," Piper tells him. "It'll be better just to wait it out. Normally, on a snow day, we binge on whatever food is in the pantry, play games, watch TV, and stay warm. It's Colorado, the sun will start to melt everything this afternoon, and things will slowly return to normal."

Sarah jumps up like she's had an idea. "We should celebrate Christmas with just the four of us. We can exchange gifts, bake cookies, and spend another evening by the fire. I don't know about the three of you, but my gifts are ready."

I have a gift for the girls back at my apartment, but my gift for Niko is technically on my phone. It could be fun to have a little mini friend-Christmas before everyone else arrives. We have the time.

I nod and look over at Piper.

"I don't see why not," she says, and looks at Niko.

"It sounds like a fantastic idea." He smiles at Sarah and gives her a little wink.

What was that?

"As long as I get to go first," Niko continues.

"Go ahead," Sarah says, with a mischievous grin. She knows something.

What are the two of them up to?

25

Niko

My heart races as we move into the lodge. Everyone is staring at me, waiting for me to make a move. I didn't plan to do this in front of everyone, and I don't have my cards. But with the way Jenni was talking earlier, I can't wait any longer. It would be cruel. Cards or no cards, I need to do this now.

"How about we all go sit down," Sarah says.

Once we're sitting around the table with our puzzle, all eyes turn to me again. I feel the anticipation in their gazes. And suddenly, nothing in the world seems more intimidating than the woman I love and her two best friends, waiting for me to give her a gift. If I've misjudged the situation, this could be bad.

"Okay," Jenni says, a nervous lilt to her voice. "I guess we just start?"

She has a smile on her face, but her eyes keep darting

around the room, as if she doesn't know what to look for. She half-heartedly holds out a hand, as if waiting for something to unwrap.

Okay, here we go. This is not a time for jokes.

"Jenni, the past few months have been some of the hardest months of my life. When you showed up at the Omorfiá, I was entirely focused on falling in step with my father and proving my worth to him. I hadn't made any time to enjoy living on the island. My world was black and white. Straight business.

"Then you showed up in a swirl of bright colors and a neon-green suitcase, looking scared to death of both the hotel and me. I realized how gray and dull my life had become. I instantly wanted to have fun with you. But you seemed so worried, that all I wanted to do was make you smile because no one should look that scared in a place like Mykonos."

She smiles. I'm sure she, too, remembers those first early days, when I refused to let her get a word in about work and instead dragged her around the island like a playmate.

"Later I realized that the reason I recognized that need in you is because it mirrored the need I felt for more joy and fulfillment," I continue. "I might not have been feeling desperate and nervous for the same reason, but I was putting everything on the line, hoping to earn Dad's approval. I was no more certain than you were that I knew what I was doing."

Jenni looks at me in shock. I've never told her any of this. "I couldn't tell," she says.

"I know, I hid it well," I tell her. I threw myself into work and adopted such a casual air of comfort that no one would have known I was overanalyzing every decision and comment from the board and my father, searching for positive feedback. "But my entire outlook changed when you arrived. I wanted to live for myself, not for someone else's approval. I realized that toiling away, doing everything to his liking, wasn't making me happy. Those two weeks we spent together were the happiest I had been in a very long time."

"Me too," Jenni admits, blushing. This isn't new information, but it still fills my heart with the confidence to keep going.

"At the time, I thought it was exploring the island that was making me feel alive. We had some great adventures. I figured I would still be happy after you returned home, hoping we would figure out how to make the fun last long-distance. But when you left? I went straight back to feeling grayscale, maybe a bit brighter than before, but nothing close to how vibrant life felt with you."

I take a deep breath. I'm about to put it all out on the line. Jenni is rapt with attention. I wish I could know what's going through her mind.

"You've been frustrated that I won't talk about your next visit to Greece, and earlier today, you asked me if I even want you to visit me there at all. And the answer is that I don't."

Her face drops. That may have been the wrong approach.

I put my hand on her knee. "Wait, hear me out," I say, pulling her gaze back to me. "I don't want you to visit Greece because I won't be there."

Now she looks confused. I sneak a glance over at Sarah, who gives me a reassuring nod.

"Jenni, if it's all right with you, I want to be here in Colorado. With you."

She smiles softly now, but it doesn't quite reach her eyes. "For how long?" She still thinks there is a goodbye looming somewhere in our near future.

"A few months or a few years? Maybe forever?" I say, not even trying to hide the emotion cracking in my voice. "I want to be wherever you are for however long you will have me."

As she digests my words, she covers her mouth with her hands and tears brim on her eyelids. There's a light in her eyes that hasn't been there all day.

"But how?" she asks. "What about the hotel? What about everything you worked for? I can't let you give that all up. I won't."

I smile with relief. Because even though she's fighting me on this, the emotion written all over her face tells me everything I need to know. She wants this, too.

"I can and I have," I tell her. I grab her hands and pull her to her feet. "I quit my job. I've already started networking here. I'll find a job, and we can be together. I want to do this."

A single tear lands on her cheek, and her smile fades. I don't know why this is so hard for her to accept. I hoped she would be jumping into my arms by now, but she still seems confused and scared. "Jenni, what's wrong?"

She swallows and squares her shoulders. "I can't let you do that for me. Your job is far more important than mine, and you've accomplished so much. You shouldn't have to start over because of me."

"Sweetheart," I say, brushing her hair behind one ear. "Nothing that I have done in Greece comes close to what you have built for yourself. You have rebuilt an entire life, and I am so proud of you. You are just starting to shine, and I want to be here to watch you accomplish all of your dreams. I want more family dinners and more time being around your friends. I love an adventure. I can't wait to explore every square mile of Colorado with you."

Jenni shakes her head. "What about Ana and your dad?"

"My dad is fine. I met with him before I left, and we finally had a genuine conversation about what I want in life. He understood, in his own way. And Ana is replacing me as the general manager. She's already thriving."

Jenni perks up with a smile as bright as the sun. "Ana is the new general manager? I need to call her and congratulate her!"

I smile. Of course, she immediately thinks of someone else

before herself. "Slow down, she's probably sleeping. But does your excitement for her mean you are going to let me move here?"

She pauses for a second, and then squeals and jumps into my arms. "Yes, of course!"

I spin her around, holding her tight, and Piper and Sarah clap when I set Jenni back down. She looks up at me. "How soon? When will you be coming back? Where are you going to live? I have so many questions."

I place my hands on her shoulders. I need her to hear me and understand. "I don't have to come back. I'm already here. I bought a one-way ticket. I want to live with you, if possible. But if you aren't ready, I'm happy to find my own place, too. You get to decide everything."

Jenni bursts out laughing, and I can't help but chuckle, even though I have no idea what I said that set her off. "What's so funny?"

"You only bought a one-way ticket ... to Colorado," she says, through fits of laughter. "And you want to move in with me."

"Yes ..." I say, still not understanding what is funny.

Jenni takes a deep breath and tries to compose herself. She looks over at Piper and Sarah and then gives me a playful look. "I'd better tell you about my gift."

"Okay," I say, excited to see what she has in store and what it has to do with the fact that I'm here for good.

Jenni takes my hands. "The last few months, I have woken up every day, excited to go and live life. And I have, don't get me wrong, but sometimes I missed you so much that I had to force myself to eat."

I'm not sure where she's going with this, but I relate to the experience.

"I couldn't take it anymore," she continues. "About a month ago, I talked to Amber.

"Since my job is so much more flexible than yours, I asked her for some extended time off. I thought I would go to Greece for a few months so we could focus on our relationship."

"I had no idea. You never said anything," I tell her. We were both taking on the responsibility of figuring things out instead of working together.

"That's not all," she says. "I bought a one-way ticket to Greece, leaving the same day you told me your flight home would be. And I'm moving out of my apartment. My sublease is up, and I've already started moving boxes to my parents' house."

She bends, clutching her stomach, laughing so hard she's barely making a sound. And suddenly I'm laughing too, wiping a tear from my eye.

"Wait, wait, wait," Piper says. "You're telling me that Niko quit his job at the hotel, bought a one-way ticket to Colorado, and planned to move into Jenni's apartment—"

"And Jenni bought a one-way ticket to Greece and let the lease end on her apartment so that she could go be with Niko at his hotel," Sarah finishes.

It's almost too ironic. We literally canceled each other out. "This is definitely a Christmas to remember," I say.

"What are we going to do?" Jenni asks.

Everything. We're going to do everything from sleeping in to grocery shopping, paying bills, and having regular date nights.

"Life," I tell her. "We're going to do life together for the first time since we met."

She wraps her arms around me. "I meant about my plane ticket and a place to live."

"You can stay here as long as you need," Piper chimes in.

"We can turn your flight into airline credit to use next summer when we visit Ana," I tell her. "And we'll find a place together. Anywhere you want."

"I would like that," she says.

"We're so happy for you," Sarah says, in tears, almost like she didn't already know this was the plan.

"Oh, I need to apologize," Jenni says, turning to the girls. "I'm so sorry that I didn't tell you what I was planning. I wanted to, but I didn't want you to think I was abandoning the inn and add to your stress. I wanted to get through the opening and was going to tell you once everything settled down."

"We would have supported you no matter what," Piper tells her. "But selfishly, I'm glad I'm not losing my best friend to the Mediterranean."

Jenni takes a deep breath, a blissful smile on her face as she turns back to me. "This could not have been more perfect."

I lean down and kiss her so passionately that I barely notice Piper and Sarah slip out of the room.

26

Piper

PINEVIEW SPRINGS, COLORADO
OPENING DAY

"Let's give them some privacy," I whisper in Sarah's ear. "I want to show you your gift."

Watching Niko and Jenni finally agree on what their life is going to look like has filled me with a longing to do the same. I know I can't make any grand gestures, like moving around the world for Sarah, but I can give her a bookshop. And for her, I think it might be just as monumental.

I lead Sarah to the kitchen. "Wait here just one minute while I shovel a path. You might want to put your boots on."

"Is my gift in the woods?" Sarah jokes.

"You'll see, just wait here." I put on my coat and gloves and open the kitchen door. There's a snow shovel propped against the wall. Thankfully, I salted these steps yesterday, so the layer of ice covering nearly everything else the eye can see isn't going to put me on my backside. I climb down, grab the shovel, and get to work.

My back burns, and my fingers grow cold as I clear a narrow path from the kitchen all the way across the gravel drive to the storage sheds. I pull out a key and unlock the shed, where I have been storing power tools. Sarah hasn't set foot in this shed for weeks because all of the decorations and furniture are in the larger shed.

I circle back to Sarah, and when I reach the kitchen, she has donned her boots, a scarf, and a hat. Jenni and Niko are standing behind her, similarly prepped for the frigid, twenty-yard walk to the shed.

I'm glad they are here. I want them to experience this, too. Jenni has been extremely helpful with collecting donations and ensuring that everyone in town was afraid for their lives if they spilled the beans to Sarah.

"We didn't want to miss this," Jenni says with a wink.

We run across to the shed. Icicles hang down from the eaves, and I have to break a thin layer of ice covering the door before it opens. We all step inside. It's not any warmer in here, but at least we are sheltered from the wind.

"Okay, close your eyes," I tell Sarah. "Seriously."

Jenni puts her hands over Sarah's face, and Sarah groans. Jenni and I both know she would peek otherwise. I pull out the bookshop sign I made from behind a stack of boxes. It's reminiscent of a vintage farm sign with a painted wooden sign hanging from a large post meant to be driven into the ground. I can't wait to see it standing in a bed of flowers outside the RV.

On the sign, I painted "The Pineview Inn Used Bookshop" in shiny black paint and used a stencil for the inn's logo beneath it.

I hold the sign up by its post and stand behind it. "Okay, open your eyes."

Jenni drops her hands, and Sarah opens her eyes, which go wide in the dim light of the shed. I wait for a response.

"The Pineview Inn Used Bookshop?" she asks, looking around. "What is this sign for?"

"It's for you! For your bookshop," I tell her. And when she still looks confused, I gently lean the sign against the wall of the shed and take a step toward her. "I know I have shot down almost every idea you've had, but Jenni helped me remember that you don't need a worrying or controlling partner. You need a partner who is willing to dream with you and problem-solve to make those dreams happen."

"I have been way too controlling since we started on this journey to open the inn. I got a little lost, emotionally, and found myself drowning in to-do lists and bank accounts. When we were traveling and had fewer responsibilities, I found it a lot easier to let go. I loved jumping at every whim and following the trail of your brilliant, artistic mind. But here, I have felt tied down, trapped by a sudden web of obligation and risk. I guess I'm still adjusting to everything."

Sarah looks like I've scolded her. Her arms are wrapped tight around her chest, and her eyebrows are pinched together, giving her features a worried look. "I know, I'm sorry! I should have realized you were under so much pressure and shut my stupid mouth instead of adding to the mountain of responsibilities," Sarah says.

"No, babe, that's not what I meant at all," I tell her. "I never want you to silence yourself because of the way I handle stress. That is a recipe for disaster. I want us to be able to talk about these things and find a middle ground where we are both comfortable. I want to show you that I respect your ideas even if I don't think we should have a bunny farm in the dining room."

She laughs, and it feels like a warm blanket, urging me to keep going.

"I hadn't thought of that, but I like it," she says with a wink.

"I also want to show you that I can dream, too. When you said you wished we could open a little bookshop on site, my immediate reaction was that we don't have space or the experience to make it work."

"A valid point," Sarah interrupts.

"Sure," I say. "But we don't have experience running an inn either, but here we are, going after it."

"And killing it," Jenni says, before Niko elbows her.

"Don't interrupt," Niko stage whispers, pretending to eat popcorn out of a movie theater tub. "I want to see what happens."

I chuckle and look Sarah straight in the eyes.

"If we can figure out running an inn, we can figure out selling books. I gathered up as many used books as I could find to get us started and thought long and hard about where we could make space."

Sarah's cheeks flush, glistening as her smile grows. "Piper, when in the world did you do all of this?"

"There may have been a few shady hand-offs late at night or behind the hardware store. Keeping this a surprise was the hardest thing I've ever done. We had to bribe so many women with offers of tea and gossip and meeting space for their weekly knitting meetings." At first, it had felt like signing my own detention note, inviting the women to use our dining space for their get-togethers. Now, however, thinking back to those encounters and how much they have shown up for us this week, I can't wait to let them hang out here. "All of these boxes are full of books for you to sort through, price, and sell. It's all yours."

Sarah looks around the shed, surveying the fifteen boxes of various sizes. "It's a dream come true," she says. She opens the first box and runs her fingers along the book spines. She pulls one out and flips the pages, inhaling the musty, earthy scent of old books. Smiling, she grabs another book and immediately flips it over to read the back cover.

"Why do I get the feeling that you're going to read eighty percent of these books before you put them on the shelves?" I ask.

"Because you know me like the back of your hand," she says, returning the books to their boxes and entwining her arms behind my neck. Sarah touches her nose to mine. "Thank you so much. I can't even tell you how much this means to me."

She kisses me, her lips soft and warm in the bleak cold that has crept into the shed while we've been talking. I can see her breath as she pulls away from me.

"Wait," she says. "Where is the space? What are we changing inside the inn?" Her face twists in confusion. We don't have space without giving up one of our few common areas.

"That's the best part," I say, my eyebrows raised to the sky. "We don't have to change anything! Let's go inside to talk about it, where we can be warm. I don't want any of us to lose our fingers or toes out here."

"Okay," Sarah says, hesitating. "But first, I need to grab one of these boxes."

She surveys the boxes of books, brushing her hand over them, as if communing with the books inside. She finally lands on a medium-sized box that, according to the label, once held jars of pickles.

"What?" she asks. "We are going to need something to keep us busy for the rest of our snow day. I'll find books in here for each of you."

Niko reaches out a hand. "Here, let me carry that over."

I did it. I made Sarah's dream come true. And there isn't a

better feeling in the world. Now, to tell her about the RV and its renovations.

27

Sarah

We settle with blankets in our cozy leather chairs in the lodge room, and Jenni starts a fire while I pester Piper about this bookshop. The anticipation is killing me. My mind has been racing nonstop. I can't believe she did this. It's the last thing I expected.

"Can you wait for two minutes?" she asks with a laugh. "I need my face to thaw out."

My excitement helped me defrost more quickly because I don't feel cold at all. I sit on the floor in front of my chair and open the box Niko carried in. I pull out the top book. It's some dime store mystery with a rugged-looking sheriff on the cover. Someone either loved or hated this book, and now more people will get to experience it right here at the inn. That's the magic of stories, they can be told and retold and never lose their spark.

"Okay," Piper says, sitting next to me and finally looking more pink than blue in the lips. "Are you ready for this?"

"Yes!" I shout, straightening up at attention. I rub my hands together in anticipation. "Please, I can't take it anymore!"

"Well, I racked my brain trying to figure out how we could fit a bookshop in here, but I just couldn't make it work without seriously compromising our other goals," Piper says.

My heart squeezes in panic. I don't want a bookshop unless it's here on the property. I don't want to leave Piper to run the inn on her own. That hardly seems fair. What we do, we do together. That has always been the plan from the beginning.

"It's not here? I don't want a storefront in town, Piper—" I start to argue, but she places a gentle hand on my shoulder. I take a deep breath, trying to work out in my head what other possibility there could be.

"When Jenni and I went to winterize the RV, it reminded me of something," she says. "You're always showing me those mobile libraries on social media where people have converted trailers and RVs into the cutest little libraries."

I didn't think she had paid attention when I showed her all of those. Just the other day, I saw one that was an old farm truck turned into a spicy-romance shop. It was painted with peppers and cacti and looked adorable. I remember wanting to find it so that I could say I had bought a book from the spicy romance truck.

"We have both struggled to part with our RV," Piper says. "It was such a huge part of our life and falling more in love. Right?"

Wait. Is she saying what I think she's saying? My chest tightens. *No.* This can't be happening. I ruined everything with my stupid grand idea, again.

Piper continues. "What if we parked the RV right here on the property and turned it into a mobile bookshop? It doesn't even have to go anywhere! I've been scouring the internet, and I can retrofit her with shelves, a sales counter, anything you need. And you could decorate it to your heart's content.

"I even marked a space out front to pour a concrete slab. We could build cedar flower beds around the RV and put up the sign. I want you to be the one to design it all."

Her eyes are full of excitement and love. And my heart sinks. It might as well have dropped right out of my chest and into my stomach because I feel like I'm going to throw up. Piper is finally dreaming big, and I have to squash it. I messed everything up.

I get up from the floor and perch at the edge of one of the chairs, my head in my hands. "Piper, we can't."

She pulls my hands away from my face, a pleading look in her eyes. "Sarah, please. Let me do this for you. I promise to make it happen. You deserve it. Not right away, of course, but we could have the shop up and running before the spring. Unless that's too soon for you to go through all the books you want to read first." She winks. I want to laugh, but my head won't stop spinning.

My heart aches for her. I don't want to tell her we can't do this because we don't own an RV anymore. It will crush her, and I can't help but think that this must be how she feels when the roles are reversed and she has to let me down.

"Piper, we can't. I want to, and I believe in your ability to make it happen. But we can't do it because I sold the RV. It's not ours anymore."

Her expression changes. Anger? Fear? Confusion? A mix of all three.

"What are you talking about? It was still parked at your parents' house a couple of days ago when I put the finishing touches on the sign."

I should have guessed my dad helped her with that sign. It

has his name all over it, from the detailed beveling to the perfect sanding. My throat constricts because it represents everything I thought I would never have—a supportive partner who enjoys spending time building with my dad, and a home with the people I care about most.

I look to Niko for reassurance. He gives me a tiny nod and then rises and leaves the room, his mug in hand. "That's because the man I sold it to is still making arrangements for storage and is paying weekly to keep it there."

Realization washes over Piper's face. Her features soften and drop. What little hope she must have had that it was just some big misunderstanding is gone. "But why did you sell it? You love the RV."

My heart is breaking into a hundred pieces seeing how much hurt and confusion this is causing her. She doesn't deserve it. But if I give Piper her gift, she'll understand why I made my decision.

Niko returns from the kitchen with a fresh cup of coffee. As he passes me, he gently presses something into my back, letting it drop silently into the chair. It's cube-shaped and the perfect size for a ring box. He must have retrieved it from my bag behind the front desk.

Thank you, I want to whisper, as I slip it into the pocket of my cargo pants.

I stand and pull her toward the fire. My hands are shaking, so I squeeze hers to steady myself. She gives me a concerned look. "Sarah, are you okay?"

I ignore her question. I'd rather get straight to the point. "I sold the RV because I found something far more important I needed to buy. It doesn't represent our past like the RV, but I hope it will represent our future."

A tear crawls down my cheek as I speak, but I don't dare let go of her hands to wipe at it. "Piper, from the moment I first saw you, my heart has felt whole. Before you, I felt like I was floating through life, trying my best to fit in and fill a certain mold. But when I met you, I knew I could blossom. Because of you, I didn't have to stay in the box I had built for myself."

I briefly consider kneeling, but that's too heteronormative, and Piper would roll her eyes. Instead, I take a step back and let go of her hands. Without breaking eye contact, I retrieve the ring box from my pocket as Piper brings a trembling hand to her mouth.

"The only reason I can dream the way I do is because I know you always have my back and keep me safe. You are my rock and biggest supporter. But none of those dreams is worth doing, unless I'm doing them with you."

My voice catches, and I swallow before I continue.

"Piper Morris, will you marry me?"

I open the ring box to reveal the sapphire-and-diamond ring I bought the very same day I sold the RV.

Piper has tears in her eyes now, too, as she lowers her left hand. "I wouldn't want to be anywhere else with anyone else in the whole world. Of course, I'll marry you."

I slide the ring onto Piper's finger, and she stares at it, her eyes gleaming. My lips tremble as I wait for her to examine how the ring looks and feels on her finger. She throws herself at me, taking me into her arms and kissing me. It's the best feeling in the world. Her arms wrap around my lower back, lifting me slightly off the ground. And I am so explosively happy.

My girl. My future wife. My forever.

Jenni wraps both of us in a bear hug, and we're all bouncing around the room screaming.

"We're getting married!"

"You're getting married!"

"We're getting married!"

If we had a dog, now would be the time when it would be jumping and chasing us around the room, trying to figure out what is happening.

"Wait," I say, stopping everyone. "We should get a dog!"

"We should get a dog!" Piper flings her arms around me. "Whatever you want."

Piper spins me around one more time before I collapse into her arms. "But what are we going to do about the bookshop if we don't have an RV?"

The fire pops, and we all stare around the circle. Niko stands casually against the back wall. We can't put books in here without losing half the seating.

"What would it cost to build a little cottage?" Niko asks.

"More than we have," Piper says.

My heart sinks. Piper did so much work to make this happen. It was such a thoughtful gift, and I hate that I can't see a way to make it work.

"I have some money left over from selling the RV," I tell Piper.

Piper spins the new ring on her left and stares down at it.

"This ring is so beautiful, Sarah. The simplicity, the blue and black hues blending so seamlessly," Piper says, fiddling with her ring. "I've truly never seen a more perfect ring." She slides it off her finger. "But I would marry you with a ring made from twine. I don't need this."

Every cell in my body rejects what she is saying. I'm not returning that ring. "No, there has to be another way. The moment I laid eyes on that ring, it sang your name. We'll figure something else out." I move to the table, pulling at the collar of my sweater. "What about converting one of the sheds? Can those things be moved?"

I'm grasping at straws. Those sheds are disgusting, but I don't know what else to do.

"Maybe, but the walls might disintegrate when we try." Piper slumps in her chair. I need to fix this. We need a miracle.

"What if I give you the money?"

All eyes in the room snap toward Niko.

Jenni speaks first, sounding genuinely confused. "What?"

Niko shrugs. "I could cover the cost of building a cottage. I have the cash. I'll give you an interest-free loan."

"That's incredibly generous, but we could never accept your offer," Piper tells Niko. "We can't mix business and friendship."

"Piper, you should take it," Jenni pleads. "Niko's not like that. He'll never hold it over you. He really wants to help. It's like his thing."

When I finally process what Niko has offered, I lean forward, putting one elbow on the arm of the chair I'm sitting in. "Are you serious about it being interest-free?" I ask.

Niko laughs. "You can pay me back on your schedule, whenever you're able to. I'm not going anywhere." He winks at Jenni and pulls her in close.

My heart melts. This little chosen family of ours is something so incredibly special.

"Piper, I know you hate asking for help, but look at how everything has turned out so far," I tell her. "We couldn't have done anything we've accomplished so far if it weren't for the help of the people around us. I think we should take Niko up on his offer."

Her eyes race over my face, searching for something. "Okay," she finally says. "You're right."

She turns to Niko. "We will pay you back, I promise. Thank you."

He nods with Jenni tight at his hip. "Don't worry about."

I feel like cheering and jumping again. "Who wants champagne?"

"Sarah, it's barely lunch time," Jenni says, laughing.

"Time has no meaning on a snow day," I call out, already on my way to the kitchen where I stashed a bottle of champagne for my Christmas Day proposal. I had a whole scene planned out, but I can't imagine things happening in a more perfect way.

28

Jenni

PINEVIEW SPRINGS, COLORADO
CHRISTMAS EVE

The roads to Pineview Springs open the day after the Polar Vortex.

Guests began arriving that afternoon, and the girls did a soft opening, checking them in as they arrived. We all decided it would be best to wait another day for the grand opening, giving the community time to thaw out.

It's now Christmas Eve, and everyone in town is gathered at the inn. The guests and townsfolk alike are dressed up as festive as can be, children in wool caps and mittens, couples draped in scarves and ear warmers. Every cheek is rosy, every smile is bright, and every heart is full.

I am incredibly proud of Piper and Sarah, and everything they have accomplished to reach this point.

My parents are here, too. My mom is thrilled with the news that Niko and I will be staying in Pineview Springs because it means she will have another person to fuss over. Niko is taking everything in stride. She has already insisted that he take one of my dad's jackets until he can buy a proper winter coat. She also gave us five separate warnings about apartment hunting. *"There are so many scams these days. I just saw on the news that people are creating fake listings to talk people into sending them a deposit."*

I smile, thinking about the gentle way Niko listens and makes her feel heard in a way that I have never been able to.

Right now, I can see Jeremy by the hot chocolate bar, catching up with a group of his high school friends, most of whom are home for the holidays. But I recognize a few who never found or needed a reason to leave. I'm happy for him. He has figured out so much more about life than I did a few years ago. I can't wait to see what he does next.

Behind them, I can see a few women from the knitting group sipping mulled wine and deep in animated conversation. I can practically smell the citrus and cinnamon from here, and I guarantee they'll be spilling everyone's secrets before the night is over. Without all of their nosiness, though, we wouldn't have made it to this night. I think their kindness has healed Piper's childhood wounds. She's no longer the little girl being excluded on the playground because of her dad's business coming to town. She's part of the heart and soul of our little town now—a local business owner.

I find the girls talking with a few guests near the firepits and give them both a hug. This is such a special night. "Are you two ready for the ceremony?"

"I think so," Piper says as her eyes dart back and forth, surveying the crowd.

"You've got this," I tell them. "I can't believe how many people still showed up on Christmas Eve."

Sarah nods, her eyes wide. It must be overwhelming to have it all finally coming together.

"Excuse me," a soft voice says from behind me. I turn

around and find Linda and Charlie LeGrande waiting patiently to talk with Piper and Sarah. I step aside, but stay within earshot.

"I'm sorry to interrupt, girls," Linda says. "But my husband has something to say to you, and I told him if he doesn't say it to your faces, he can't have any of the delicious treats you've provided."

"Oh, okay," Sarah says. "Hi, Charlie, I'm Sarah. We've never officially met."

"It's nice to meet you," he tells her, shifting his weight on his feet. "I used to work with your dad. He's a good man."

"Her dad is around here somewhere, you'll have to say hello," Piper says, her arms crossed in front of her chest.

"Well, I was just telling Linda that I was wrong," Charlie says, his cheeks turning red. "You've done a beautiful job with the inn and created a great atmosphere for the town to celebrate together."

Piper and Sarah both look at him, eyebrows raised.

"Thank you, Charlie," Sarah responds. "That is very kind of you."

"Piper," Charlie continues. "I'm sorry that I have given you a hard time. I'm an old man, holding on to old grudges, and I tend to get carried away. I'm glad you are here."

Piper bites her lip. I can see gratitude in the way her eyes soften. "I really appreciate that. Change is hard. I've been going through a lot of change myself. But I promise you that we care deeply about Pineview Springs and always will."

I smile, grateful that Piper gets to close that chapter. I turn to look for Niko and nearly crash into him.

"Hi. There you are," Niko says. "Do you have a minute? I have a surprise for you."

"Another one? Are you dragging me to the mistletoe?" I ask and take the steaming cup from him, smelling a hint of peppermint. "How many surprises are you expecting one girl to handle?"

"This is the last one, I promise. And it's not mistletoe, but that does remind me that we need to find it later. Follow me." Niko takes my hand, and I do as he says.

A sense of belonging fills me as our hands intertwine. Niko is here, and he's staying here because he wants to be with me. There is no better feeling in the world.

I walk with him toward the front of the inn, where a firetruck is getting ready to pull away down the long drive. The local station decorated one of its engines, and firefighters have been giving festive "sleigh" rides all evening.

When the truck pulls away, I see a blacked-out sedan idling behind it. I half-expect Sophia, Niko's driver in Mykonos, to open the door and give me her trademark smile. But I remind my brain that she is a world away, already celebrating Christmas morning with her grandchildren. Instead, a bald man exits the driver's side and opens the passenger door for one of the most classically beautiful women I have ever seen.

"Jenni," Niko says. "I would love for you to meet my mother, Daphne."

My heart skips a beat. Immediately, I enter hyperdrive, vacillating between wanting to make a good first impression and owning the fact that I am already completely smitten with her just from the few stories I've heard. "Hi! Oh, my gosh. It's so nice to meet you!" I tug on the hem of my sweater and toss my hair over my shoulder before putting a hand out to greet her.

Instead of taking it, Daphne pulls me into an all-encompassing hug, a stark contrast from the way Niko's dad scoffed down his nose the first time he met me. Now I can see who Niko really takes after. He might share eyes with his father, but he shares a heart with his mother.

"Jenni, it's so amazing to finally meet you," Daphne says, pulling away. "And I have to thank you."

"Thank me?" I can't think of a single thing she needs to thank *me* for. I don't even know why she's here. We're supposed to be visiting her in California next week.

"For bringing my little boy back," she says, hugging me again. I sneak a peek at Niko over her shoulder. His cheeks have turned bright red.

"Mom, I'm not your little boy anymore," Niko says. "But I'm happy to be back, too."

"When Niko called to tell me the good news, I had to catch the next flight here. I know you're coming my way soon, but if my Niko is going to live here, I need to see it. That way, I can picture your daily life and know that you are happy and safe."

She pinches Niko's cheek, and he rolls his eyes bashfully. I want to burst from the cuteness, watching their relationship play out in person. I have heard so much about the kind and loving woman who raised Niko by herself in California, because she wanted him to have a world of possibilities beyond the two high-society families he came from in Greece.

Niko's maternal family is even more successful and wealthy than his father's, something to do with petroleum. It would intimidate the crap out of me if I didn't already know how down-to-earth he is.

"Just knowing that you are a two-hour flight from Los Angeles instead of halfway across the world makes me feel like I won the motherhood lottery," Daphne says.

The way she says it, I get the feeling Niko hasn't told her about his new job yet. Niko called a friend from grad school the day after our snow-in. It only took him three minutes to invite Niko to join their startup in Los Angeles, which makes luggage and donates bags to foster children across the United States. Niko will travel to L.A. monthly for staff meetings and, hopefully, travel around the U.S. to coordinate with various donors and welfare organizations. With my job's flexibility, I plan to go right alongside him and spend as few days apart as possible.

As Daphne goes in for another hug with her son, Sarah comes on the loudspeaker to announce that the tree lighting will take place in ten minutes.

"Let's take your bags inside and get you something to eat," Niko tells his mom, picking up her bag. "We'll see you out there, Jenni?"

"Yes, I have to go make sure the Harpers are where they are supposed to be anyway," I say. "Daphne, I'm so happy you're here."

I wander back through the crowd under the market lights and cool winter air. This night is perfect.

I find Mr. and Mrs. Harper near the fudge table. He's pretty cozy in a wheelchair, still not quite sturdy enough on his feet after the stroke. He is wrapped up in yet another of the knitting group's blankets and wearing a sturdy trapper hat that looks like it has seen more Colorado winters than I have. Mrs. Harper is dressed in a cozy overcoat and jeans, with snow boots that reach up to her knees. They are laughing and smiling with each other as they eat Sarah's fudge.

"Hi," I say, as I approach the Harpers. "Are you both ready to go?"

Piper and Sarah have asked the Harpers to light the trees as a part of the grand opening. It only felt right, considering how important it was to the girls to carry on the Harpers' legacy.

"Hello, Miss Swanson," Mr. Harper says, his asymmetrical smile beaming. "I just saw your parents, and they told me all about your new job. I always thought you had a knack for marketing when you worked at the front desk. No one upsold the Pineview Inn like Jenni Swanson."

My face flushes at the compliment. I had forgotten about

that. In high school, when I worked at the front desk, I used to keep track of how many guests I could get to rebook at check-out. I had a sticker chart and everything. Now, I get to help independent hotels all over the world bring guests through their front doors. It's funny how that came full circle.

"You are too kind," I say, squeezing his hand. "I've been happy since I left Chicago. That life just wasn't for me."

"I'm just glad you figured it out before wasting any more time," Mrs. Harper tells me. "Some people spend their whole lives chasing dreams that don't fit."

An alarm on my watch buzzes, telling me we have two minutes to take our place by the tree. I help the Harpers make their way over, and then I find Niko, his mom, and my parents all standing in the front row of the crowd. Joining them, I take Niko's gloved hand in mine.

"Hello everyone," Piper says on the microphone. "We are so happy to have you all here, especially on Christmas Eve. We appreciate your flexibility with Colorado's fickle weather."

The crowd laughs, and Piper hands the microphone to Sarah.

"We are so grateful for all of the support as we reopen the Pineview Inn. Our vision for this inn is not only to carry on a legacy of hospitality and Pineview spirit, but also to introduce new ways for the community and our guests to come together. We hope you enjoy the food and drink, and we invite you to stay for s'mores and sleigh rides."

Piper hands two extension cords to Mr. and Mrs. Harper and then takes the mic back from Sarah. "We now want to acknowledge the Harpers, who ran this inn for decades and probably employed at least half of us here at one time or another." A cheer goes up from the crowd, and tears well in my eyes. "Our deepest hope is to continue what they started. Please join us in a countdown before they light the tree."

We all chant: "*Three! Two! One!*"

Mrs. Harper helps her husband hold his end steady, and they plug in the tree. White twinkle lights illuminate the Christmas tree, causing the shiny ornaments to sparkle and shimmer. The crowd cheers, and I know that everyone feels what I'm feeling in the air. That magical feeling of a new start and the promise of happy futures, exciting changes, and most importantly, the stability of being surrounded and supported by the people I love.

Epilogue | Niko

The Pineview Inn has undergone a complete transformation. Elegant silk ribbons drape every banister and railing, bouquets of lilies and fern clippings adorn each table, and a wooden archway, built by one of the brides' fathers, stands on the patio, decorated in greenery, flowers, and lace. It's the perfect focal point for the autumn mountain ceremony.

The bright yellow aspen trees, deep red oaks, and striking orange maple trees could not have been placed more perfectly for the outdoor venue. I understand why Piper and Sarah planned an October wedding. This day is everything one pictures a fall wedding to be. It's perfect for what I have planned later, too.

Jenni is helping the girls get ready, so I'm enjoying the ambiance on my own for now. I imagine she's bouncing back and forth between the two separate bridal rooms, helping Piper with her hair and Sarah with her dress. Her two best friends are getting married, and she must be in heaven. I know she'll look as gorgeous as the backdrop when she finally joins my side. Meanwhile, guests are milling about the grounds, sipping apple-flavored cocktails and waiting for the ceremony to begin. I spy Jenni's parents across the lawn and head to join them.

"Niko, hi!" Rebecca calls as I approach. "How are you? How was your trip to Chicago?"

I haven't seen them since I returned from Chicago last week, where I met with a foster youth program to arrange a donation of 5,000 duffel bags for the children who come through their doors. Most people don't know that foster kids have to carry everything they own with them when they move from one placement to another. And far too many of them end up using trash bags. Our company is trying to change that, one luggage sale at a time.

"It was great. I had a successful meeting and ate *way* too much pizza. What else could I want?"

Jenni joined me in Chicago at the last minute. She was very apprehensive, given her past, but we ended up spending a wonderful weekend making new memories in a city that once held so much pain for her. I loved being a part of creating new memories.

"Where are you two off to next, then?" Jenni's dad asks.

"Not sure," I say. "We may stick around for a while. We haven't been home longer than a few weeks recently."

"Good, we'll be happy to have you here, especially for the holidays," he responds.

Jenni and I rented a small two-bedroom home in Pineview Springs that overlooks the lake last January. We have a guest room so my mom can visit, and we love taking morning walks along the water, coffee in hand.

We wanted to stay close so that when we aren't traveling, we can spend as much time as possible with Piper, Sarah, and

Jenni's family. We've traveled to ten different cities together since Christmas, and over the summer, we even went back to visit the Omorfiá so that Jenni could get her fix of Greek pastries and, of course, Ana and Alexander.

She is thriving at work, taking on new clients every month. One of my favorite things to do is sit at the table after dinner and listen to her brainstorm new ways to market each unique property. It reminds me of my time at the hotel. I'm still proud of what we accomplished there, but I don't miss it.

"It looks like everyone is gathering on the patio," Rebecca says. "We'd better hurry so we don't lose our seats."

We make our way to the rows of chairs and take our seats in the third row, right behind both families. As the crowd settles, I feel a tap on my shoulder. "Is this seat taken?"

I turn and find Jenni, wearing a gorgeous, burnt-orange chiffon bridesmaid dress. I am blown away by how stunning she looks with her brown waves gently stirring in the breeze. "It's not, but don't you have to be in the procession as the maid of honor to not one, but both the brides?"

"I do," she says, sheepishly. "I was just hoping I could drop my bag here. Once we get to the front, I'll be able to come sit."

"Good, go knock everyone dead," I tell her. She leans down and gives me a quick kiss before returning to the dining room of the inn, where the processional group is assembled.

Piper comes down the aisle first, with both of her parents on either side of her. She's dressed in a white pantsuit and deep navy blue suede loafers. She looks stunning. Next, Sarah approaches, wearing a champagne-colored wedding dress flowing around her as she walks. She is linking arms with both her parents as she holds a giant cascading bouquet of orange, white, and yellow lilies that complements her glowing smile perfectly. I have never seen someone this happy to walk down the aisle.

AFTER A CEREMONY that left every single audience member in tears, the chairs are cleared off the patio for the party while everyone eats dinner on the lawn. Once the cake is cut and respectfully smashed in the brides' faces, the crowd moves back to the dance floor.

A live band plays as we all move together under the moonlit sky. The inn is fully booked with those celebrating the wedding, so we don't have to worry about a curfew or noise complaints. We can party the night away.

Long after midnight, after the brides have settled in their honeymoon suite and the guests have all turned in or gone home, Jenni and I are alone on the dance floor. We sway to nothing but the sound of crickets and a crisp fall breeze rustling the golden aspen leaves. It's time.

"I have something for you," I tell her.

"Oh yeah? What else could we possibly need on a night like this?" she asks, her voice soft and dreamy, as she lays her head on my chest.

The last time I planned a grand gesture, I accidentally caused Jenni to question everything about our relationship, so this time, I'm keeping it simple. I step away from her and get down on one knee.

"Jenni, the past nine months, I have only grown more certain every day that I want you by my side for all of life's adventures.

"Will you marry me?"

I hold out a simple, elegant ring that Ana helped me pick out months ago. It's a teardrop diamond surrounded by pink sapphires on a gold band.

"Niko! Am I dreaming? Is this really happening right now?" Jenni squeals.

"Yes, sweetheart, it's really happening," I say, smiling up at her, knowing that she needs a little reassurance. It's just part of who she is, and I'll make it my life's purpose to assure her of my love over and over if she lets me.

"Yes," she answers. "All the adventures. All the time. As long as they are with you."

I slip the ring onto her finger and pull her close. "Thank you," I tell her.

"For what?"

"For being exactly who you are and filling my life with sunshine."

Jenni guides my chin down so our faces come closer together. "Thank you for always being a safe place for me to land. I don't know if you'll ever understand how it feels to know that I'm loved completely and wholly, no matter what."

I meet her words with a kiss. Pulling away, I lift her hand and guide her into a twirl one more time, slow and steady, because I want to remember the way she looks tonight for the rest of my life.

Leave A Review

Wow! I can't believe I live in a world where you just read my book! I hope you loved it. Thank you from the bottom of my heart. If you enjoyed the book, please consider leaving a review on Goodreads, StoryGraph, or Amazon! Reviews help spread the word and are essential for indie authors. It also brings a bit of sunshine to my day anytime my book is shared!

Acknowledgments

I first want to thank everyone who read and enjoyed *Accidental Getaway* and encouraged me to keep going. Writing is such a vulnerable endeavor that every message, comment, and photo of you reading filled my soul. Thank you from the bottom of my heart.

Thank you, Mom and Dad! As mentioned in the dedication, thank you for always watching cheesy holiday movies to inspire this book. Which Hallmark actors do you think could play Jenni, Niko, Piper, and Sarah? Also, thank you for being the first people who ever told me I should write books. I didn't mention that last time (sorry!), but your belief in me has always been invaluable.

To my husband and children, thank you for always putting up with my rambling about my stories. Thank you for letting me work during soccer practices or by the pool. Thank you for constantly bragging about me and my books. I love you!

Kylee, thank you for reading the very first versions of this book and believing in this story. Your help is the only way I got this book finished in time for Christmas.

Pirate Queens, Rachel, Emily, and the Tenacious Writers group, thank you for always being a supportive environment, for pushing me as a writer, for holding my hand when I needed it, and for cheering me on. I'm right here cheering for you at the top of my lungs! You are all incredible!

About the Author

Molly Gray has traveled the world, but still feels most at home inside a good rom-com. A former journalist, Molly now spends her time being a mom to her three kids and writing romance books with an adventurous streak. On her desk, you can almost always find chips and salsa. She also loves hiking, crocheting, coaching her kids' sports teams, and reading...of course.

Website: http://www.mollygraybooks.com
   Instagram and TikTok: @mollygraywrites

Also by Molly Gray

Accidental Getaway